H₁

SCOTTISH SHORT STORIES

SCOTTISH SHORT STORIES 1974

Preface by
CLIFFORD HANLEY

COLLINS
LONDON 1974

William Collins Sons & Co Ltd

London · Glasgow · Sydney · Auckland
Toronto · Johannesburg

First published 1974

Published with the support of the Scottish Arts Council

ISBN 0 00 221891 7

Set in Monotype Garamond
Made and printed in Great Britain by
William Collins Sons & Co Ltd Glasgow

CONTENTS

CONTENTS

PREFACE

The short story has suffered from trends in the publishing trade in recent decades. Commercial pressure has struck down many of the eminent magazines which once served the art and pleased a wide public.

There are signs now – faint signs, it is true – that things may get better. The magazine industry never stands still, and writers and readers may hope that the short story will rise again, and spread, and flourish.

In the meantime, we offer this volume as evidence that the beast is not at all dead. It is the second short story book sponsored by the Scottish Arts Council. The first was popular and successful and showed clearly that the idea was a good one.

The Scottish Arts Council invited Scottish writers known and unknown to compete for inclusion in the book, and the weight of entries proved that the writers at least are there, willing and able.

The selection team, consisting of James Allan Ford, Philip Ziegler and myself, had a hard and even contentious job in reducing that weight to a book that would be both manageable and balanced. Plenty of good material had to be discarded simply in the cause of balance. This is both sad and reassuring.

Volume Two *is* a nice balance, we believe. It has tragedy and frivolity and nostalgia and suspense, and it has short and long. We are grateful particularly to Robert Buckie, Alan Spence and Fred Urquhart for agreeing to cut their original versions to fit into the shape of the book. But we thank all

the writers, In and Out, for their enthusiastic support, and
we commend them to you, dear reader, for your pleasure.

CLIFFORD HANLEY

TOM BUCHAN

TWO FOR IMMORTALITY

GREAT UNCLE CONRAD was the first dead man I ever saw.

'You are old enough to go to your Great Uncle Conrad's funeral,' my father said, conferring adulthood upon me.

Great Uncle Conrad was my father's uncle by marriage. A miser. He hoarded years as well as money. He was nearly ninety.

'You are coming to Great Uncle Conrad's funeral,' my father said.

When we were very young and there was still hope that Great Uncle Conrad would die on time and leave us some of his fortune, we were taken to see him once a year, usually just before Christmas, and paraded before him to jog his memory. He lived on the other side of the river in a large detached red-sandstone mansion. We took the ferry which was the only enjoyable part of the visit. It was obvious to me, though not apparently to my father, that Great Uncle Conrad did not enjoy these visits. He always behaved with great nervousness, stumbling through theological conversations with my father. He hid his cigarettes because he feared the judgment of God and knew that there was always a chance that my father's testimonial might count for something on the other side. But we were always able to spot at least one packet of cigarettes. It was like hunt the thimble:

if Great Uncle Conrad's packet of illicit cigarettes wasn't behind some ornament or in the brass coal-scuttle, then he had not had time or had forgotten to hide it and it was still burning a hole in the pocket of his saffron dressing gown.

Once we spotted a half-bottle of whisky in the coal-scuttle and Great Uncle Conrad was scandalised.

When we were older and were sent to visit Great Uncle Conrad on our own, he abandoned all hypocrisy and signed us on as fellow conspirators, fishing a green packet of Woodbines from his dressing gown and offering us one before taking one himself. He would hold it awkwardly between his fragile fingers and smoke it slowly and carefully like a reefer and always with a slightly guilty air as if it was a very daring thing to do at his age.

Great Aunt Etta was a small woman, one year older than Great Uncle Conrad and, like him, hunchbacked with age. Family gossip had it that she had married him for his money and the good life and had therefore got her deserts by enjoying neither. Like a gambler who has lost a wager. Over the years she had presumably reconciled herself to her just punishment and come to love Great Uncle Conrad, for she had appropriated his queerer characteristics and twittered round his armchair solicitously. My mother was sure she smoked Woodbines and drank whisky on the sly. Neither of them had ventured outside the house for decades – all sorties were undertaken by a succession of dishonest and impertinent cooks and housekeepers who stole the whisky and fiddled the housekeeping money. On one of our unaccompanied visits my brother and I had to stay for lunch and were each served a sardine on a finger of underdone toast followed by a tablespoonful of tapioca which my brother couldn't bring himself to eat because it reminded him of frogspawn. This caused great mirth when it was reported at home and the story passed into family mythology.

Being staunch Puritans, my family found anything to do with bodily functions amusing. My father was a general practitioner into the bargain. Sex and excretion were reminders of man's fallen state. One was allowed to be quite frank and even facetious about them as long as one was doctrinally correct. Death came into this category and could be announced and discussed with suppressed hilarity. Dying was charged with joyful emotion for those around the bed. Death was funny in itself. The relations were happy at the departed's good luck in going to be with Jesus. Someone else's death was also God's kindly advance notice of one's own impending journey to well-deserved immortality. A funeral was an instructive occasion, not an opportunity to display sentiment. One did not grieve for the dead, one rejoiced for them and judicious theological banter was perfectly in order. Uncle Conrad's death was especially instructive and amusing because of his mouth-watering wealth.

'Lay up treasure in heaven,' my father said.

'Fancy having to leave behind all that money!' my mother said.

'Lay up treasure in heaven,' my father said, 'where neither moth nor rust corrupteth.'

'He never did a day's work in his life,' my mother said. Great Uncle Conrad had converted one hundred thousand pounds into two hundred thousand pounds by being a sleeping partner in a firm of umbrella manufacturers.

'Johnny doesn't have any black shoes,' my mother said, looking at me affectionately because she knew how reluctant I was to go to Great Uncle Conrad's funeral. I invited such sadism. I realised that it had been she who had put my father up to it.

'He can wear an old pair of mine,' my father said.

My father looked out an old pair of black shoes. They

were several sizes too large for me as was only to be expected. They certainly looked funereal enough. The uppers were criss-crossed with dry wrinkles and creases and the heels were worn down at different angles from my own shoes. I felt completely disorientated in them.

'They look fine,' my mother said, her lips pursed appraisingly.

The long, thin toe-caps jutted out far beyond the wide turn-ups of my school flannels. It was weird, looking down at my toe-caps and realising that my toes weren't in there.

As my father and I drove across the city I imagined myself wittily recounting the macabre details of the funeral to my school friends the following morning, but by the time we were chugging across the river in the ferry all my enjoyment of the trip had evaporated and my stomach was beginning to feel distinctly queasy. By the time we drew up outside Great Uncle Conrad's imposing mansion I felt shaky with nausea and anticipation. As we crunched up the drive, me in my outsize shoes, I became aware that the house had a festive air about it. The windows sparkled. Smart black limousines and family saloons were arriving continuously and emptying groups of cheerful relations. Uncle Willie – he was a lay preacher in his spare time – arrived in the old van he used for transporting his flannelgraph and amplifying equipment from gospel-meeting to gospel-meeting. The house vibrated with scarcely-controlled gaiety. All it needed was strings of bunting, flags and paper decorations and posters of Great Uncle Conrad pasted up on the window, champagne, and a rock group blasting away on the lawn.

Great Aunt Etta was shaking hands and kissing above the fruitcake.

'Poor Conrad. Poor Conrad,' she murmured. Like her husband she found social intercourse nerve-racking. An almost insupportable strain.

'Poor Conrad,' she giggled. 'He was so frightened of dying.'

The drawing-room was packed. There were one or two solemn strangers who turned out to be directors of the umbrella firm and, standing in a corner by themselves, the lawyer and banker who, six months later, were discovered to have embezzled between them a hundred grand of Great Uncle Conrad's assets. I felt an impostor in my cast-off shoes and couldn't bring myself to capitalise on my sudden and unusual popularity as the only representative present of the rising generation. None of my cousins was there. My uncles and aunts just had to smile and make the best of my father's diplomatic *coup* in producing me in full mourning rig-out. Uncle Willie waved to me merrily from the other side of the room. Uncle Willie spoke at open-air meetings for which he was billed as the Revd Willie Fraser. To the children he was 'Uncle Willie'.

'How many books in the Bible?' he used to start off his talk. 'A prize of one leather-bound New Testament to the boy or girl who can tell Uncle Willie how many books there are in the Holy Bible. Put your hand up, the boy or girl who can tell me how many books there are in the Bible.' And he would start counting them off on his fingers: 'Genesis, Exodus, Leviticus, Numbers, Deuteronomy . . . ?'

A cheery soul, he stood munching Great Aunt Etta's damp chocolate biscuits.

'. . . Duty-ronomy . . . Joshwa, Judges, Ruth . . .'

Now and then one or two of the mourners would leave the room and reappear after an interval of a few minutes. It was only towards the end of the tea-party that I guessed they must be paying their last respects to the earthly remains of Great Uncle Conrad.

Uncle Willie came up to me with a plate of madeira cake.

'Would you like to have a look at the old boy?'

'OK,' I said, horrified at my jauntiness.

'Come on then. They're just going to screw him down.'

And indeed the undertaker's man was hovering at the dining-room door with a screwdriver in his hand.

The rich coffin lay on the dining-room table. Its lid stood upright against the wall. My eyes swept the room desperately, looking for a packet of Woodbines hidden among the bric-à-brac.

I had steeled myself to take a quick nonchalant glance but found myself having to lean over the table in order to see what was in the coffin. I held my breath so as not to inhale any odour. Uncle Willie laid his hand on my shoulder as I almost overbalanced. With a magician's flourish the undertaker's man whisked off a lace-bordered napkin to reveal Great Uncle Conrad's head. His upper chest was dressed in a brown-striped pyjama jacket. Great Uncle Conrad's mouth gaped open. No one had bothered to tie up his jaw. I stared down past his gleaming dentures and straight down into his solidified pink throat at a stiff, shiny epiglottis which stuck out from his throat, forlorn and distant and unmoistened with living saliva . . .

I went through the rest of the proceedings in a morbid daze. My eyes fanatically memorised every detail of the funeral. The polished brightwork of the hearse. The clumsy manoeuvres with the ornate coffin. The wet narrow hole of the grave. The earthy impedimenta of canvas, planks, ropes and spades. Uncle Willie tipping the cemetery workers with crisp new pound notes. But then and for the rest of that day my spinning imagination was busy with Great Uncle Conrad's dry epiglottis in its lonely *rigor mortis*, the taut, winged skin of his upper palate. And with the fact that he had been buried in his pyjamas.

After the funeral Uncle Willie came to our house for a large celebratory lunch. The main course was roast beef and brussels sprouts. During the meal he suggested to my father that we all take the rest of the day off and go down to Largs and hold an impromptu open-air gospel meeting. It was early closing day, after all.

'And the boys can go to that zoo place when we're finished.'

'It won't be open in November,' said my mother. 'Not on a weekday.'

We drove to Largs in Uncle Willie's van. My father and Uncle Willie unloaded the equipment in the seafront car-park where they usually staged their meetings – Uncle Willie knew one of the town councillors who was a good evangelical Christian. While I held on to my youngest brother on the periphery of the crowd, Uncle Willie stood in the back of the van holding the mike like a pop-star. My brother started to jump up and down at the sight of a large tortoise which a shivering girl in a bikini and fur-coat was walking along the top of the sea-wall as an advertisement for the miniature zoo.

'Lookit! Lookit!' he shouted, jumping up and down at the end of my arm.

'Tortoise,' I said. '130 years old.'

GIANT AFRICAN TORTOISE 130 YEARS OLD NATURE'S WONDERLAND THE LITTLE ZOO WITH THE BIG REPUTATION IF YOU ARE NOT SATISFIED JUST ASK FOR YOUR MONEY BACK ONLY ONE DISSATISFIED CUSTOMER SINCE 1954.

'How many books in the Bible?' boomed Uncle Willie's amplified voice.

A couple emerged from the concrete exit of the miniature zoo dragging a screaming child between them.

'What did you see?' asked the harassed woman. 'The woolly monkeys, the ducks, the lambies – the wee sheepie mehs?'

'What think ye of Christ?' boomed Uncle Willie.

SPEEDBOAT TRIPS BY POLARIS PATERSONS DECK CHAIRS HELICAT MK VIII PHOTOS COMPLETED IN 3 MINUTES 4 FOR 3/– 4 DIFFERENT POSES DEVELOPED WHILE YOU WAIT ELECTRONIC RIFLES.

'Behold the Lamb of God which taketh away the sins of the world,' shouted Uncle Willie. 'John one and twenty-nine. Did you know that George Washington was murdered? One of the late Presidents of the United States of America. When he was very seriously ill the doctors prescribed bleeding. Bleeding! As quickly and as fastly as possible they drained him of his pure blood. Now, modern science tells us that pure blood is the chemical basis of life . . .'

NEW THIS SEASON MALABAR SQUIRREL VERY TAME & FRIENDLY LATE ARRIVALS COTTON-TOP MARMOSETS WOOLLY MONKEY 5 FT MONITOR LIZARD.

The girl in the bikini had taken the tortoise in and now emerged on the parapet with a monkey on a chain. My brother started to jump up and down again. The monkey spun itself round and round on the end of the chain.

'The saving blood of Jesus,' Uncle Willie shouted into the mike as he worked himself up to his climax.

It began to rain: a soft, penetrating drizzle. After two or three youths had declared themselves for Christ and been counselled by my father in the back of the van, we packed up. Uncle Willie had an open-air meeting in Airdrie that evening. It was getting dark. There was no time to visit the miniature zoo. We drove home through Kilbirnie and Lochwinnoch and Johnstone. When we arrived home my mother met us on the doorstep with an eager grin of welcome.

'President Kennedy's been shot,' she said.

After the TV bulletins I went up to my bedroom and wrote it all down in my diary with the pompous intensity of youth.

2

SUNDAY IN THE NEW TOWN

To walk through the greyness and stillness of a wet Sunday morning in the New Town of Edinburgh at any time of the year is to be reminded irresistibly of autumn, of falling leaves and impending hibernation.

Many of the Georgian carriageways which traverse these two square miles of elegance and decay are still surfaced with small blocks of granite. Damp with rain and catching the thin northern light they recede from the eye of the pedestrian like tiny gravestones – to the right, to the left and up the centre. Almost the only colour set against the long, grimly embellished blocks of residences is provided by the traffic lights which twinkle at intersections, like exotic birds in a petrified forest.

On a wet Sunday, and before the church bells ring, the only sign of life is a face looking down its nose from behind white astragals, a listless dog by a gaunt lamp-post, an ill-informed stranger waiting for an Edinburgh Corporation bus which does not run on the Sabbath.

Every Sunday at half past ten, Douglas Grant walked along Great Charlotte Street from his flat to the corner shop which sold, as if by Divine indulgence, newspapers, milk and morning rolls. For him, this was at once a routine and a ceremony. He preferred to avoid the crowds of church-goers who took to the New Town streets at ten to eleven.

As it was fully five hours before he went to his newspaper office, he wore his Sunday undress uniform of sweater and jeans, old brown shoes, and comfortable pair of spectacles spliced with sticking plaster.

His footsteps rang on the grey flagstones, like a warder's in the corridor of a prison. Ahead, at a distant intersection, a solitary car moved downhill through the New Town towards the docks and the iron-grey sea. Even its quiet engine was enough to disperse the pre-church silence.

It was then that Douglas saw the girl, far ahead, beyond where the car had been. A girl, loitering desolately, just wandering about on the pavement. He continued to walk towards her, carefully minding his own business, but none the less aware that on that wet Sunday morning in the greyest part of the city the two of them were the only moving, warm-blooded creatures in sight.

As he watched her, she suddenly bent forward, to become a stricken statue, staring at the street in front of her. Douglas approached, automatically assessing the trouble like any ordinary reporter beginning a story. He decided she was looking for something, peering at the tiny granite grave-stones – peering, because at the same time she was crying.

In the streets of Edinburgh it is customary to hurry away from displays of emotion amongst strangers, but this was Sunday, and no one else was in sight, save for a small black cat which now approached, treading delicately in the Georgian gutter.

It was because of his upbringing, Douglas supposed, that he was unable to help himself. He passed her by, hesitated, turned back towards her, and heard himself ask like a sort of urban shop-walker: 'Can I help you, by any chance?'

The girl straightened up and faced him, pushing back the hair that had fallen loose. It was real, startling auburn hair, the colour of old oak leaves in late autumn.

'I've lost something,' she said. 'But that's not why I'm crying.'

She had a round face, lightly freckled; the sort of mouth that can speak cruelly to maximum effect. Although her eyes were blurred with anger or grief, they still seemed to search, assess and conclude, all in the single glance she threw him. He looked at her left hand and saw that she wasn't wearing a ring.

'Is it polite to ask what you've lost?'

'I've dropped a contact lens out of one eye.'

He studied her face to see if she were joking. 'Which eye?'

'The left one. That's why the tears are getting out.'

Douglas bent and began systematically to scan the pavement, a pavement of smooth grey Caithness flagstones, the divisions between them infilled by grit.

Church bells began to ring.

Edinburgh is a great city for churches, and its religious devotions are, if nothing else, obvious. Doors opened, and New Town residents began to punctuate the wide grey emptiness of the streets, the women in fancy hats despite the rain, the family men in dark overcoats, assuming that particular expression of mild amiability that even the most cold-blooded of Writers to the Signet manage to maintain for attendance at church. Naturally, these passers-by stared at the young man in the casual clothes, not dreaming of asking what he could be doing on his knees in the damp roadway, at the feet of a pale red-haired girl who appeared to be crying.

After a long ten minutes of scrutiny, while the bells rang for morning worship, Douglas found something. It lay translucent and delicate as a baby's finger nail, about a foot and a half from the kerb. The grey light from the sullen sky was just enough to show it up, a husk of bluish pink, pathetically fragile against the coarse granite.

'That's it, isn't it?'

She came across quickly, squatting on her heels, close enough for her shoulder to touch his.

She said, 'You clever bastard.'

She put out a hand and, with a slender thumb and fore-finger, retrieved her contact lens.

'Come on,' she said. 'Let's get out of here, before we get trodden underfoot. Come on. Come with me.'

She walked across the pavement and up two steps to a black Georgian door which carried all the original brass-work, including a huge knocker in the form of a sphinx with upswept earpieces. She took a key from her pocket and inserted it in the brassbound lock. The heavy door swung open into darkness that was like the hold of a ship. The hall light, shaped like a lantern with sides of brown glass, showed Douglas a tall Chinese vase filled with bullrushes, and a dark oak staircase with an ugly banister leading to an upper floor.

The girl began to climb. She held out a hand and Douglas took it. It was a warm hand, firm and full of perplexing intent, and it drew him confidently upwards to a dim landing and into a sitting room whose gigantic windows overlooked the street.

As in all of the house he had seen so far, the prevailing colour was brown – or shades of brown – even to the astragals on the windows.

'Stay here,' she said. 'I'm going to fix my lenses. I shall either put one in or take one out. Then I'll see you better. Did you know they cost forty pounds?'

She went out and left him in a silence which seemed to gather intensity from dark upholstery, faded cameo portraits round the black marble fireplace, a brass urn of copper beech leaves, a plain black cross – without any figure – implanted in a lump of green marble. More than anything else, the room was dominated by the slow tick of a big antique clock.

On a side table stood a photograph of the girl in a silver frame. She sat primly in academic robes, her hair caught back close to her head. The photographer had managed to capture a striking impression of the radiant idealism of graduation day.

Her face, Douglas thought, was subtly different now.

As he studied the portrait she entered the room behind him. She had brushed her hair so that it fell loose, a great auburn mane, quite unlike the photograph. Her eyes looked different without any make-up – smaller and harder.

She shut the heavy brown door behind her and came straight to him, putting both hands on his shoulders and leaning her weight on him, so that he was obliged to sit down on the big brown sofa. As he held her there, be-wildered, she put her mouth over his.

It was a deliberate, calculated act – like someone who goes to a coat hanger and hangs a coat on it.

It was a long kiss. The thin lips were moist and anxious. When she drew back a little she whispered:

'The church bells are still ringing.'

They were. The grey air and the empty street outside were full of the sound of bells. He fancied he could even hear the deep boom of the big bell of St Giles Cathedral from far up on the ancient crag of the Old Town.

In the velvet twilight of the room the movements of the young man and the girl on the sofa lowered them deeper into the swollen cushions. The clock on the mantelpiece marked the passing seconds like an old person clicking his tongue in disapproval. After a few minutes Douglas became aware that the ticking had stopped. He jerked his head and shoulders round in what was now an electric silence.

'It's all right,' she said between her teeth. 'It often stops.

It seems to pick up vibrations. The bloody thing's about a hundred and fifty years old.' She put a forearm up behind his neck and hauled his face down again, locking his head in the crook of her elbow. The clock remained stopped.

'It's Sunday,' he kept thinking. 'It's Sunday.'

Rain came in a heavy shower of pear-shaped drops, striking sullenly at the great windows. As he turned his face for more air he caught sight of curtains in an upper flat across the street, moving in a sudden swirl.

'They can see us from across the street,' he panted, although he no longer felt concerned.

'So what?' Her eyes were half masked by the upper lids. 'It'll brighten their Sunday for them. If they dare to watch. And if they're caught watching by someone else they will draw attention to what they saw, and say, isn't it disgusting. And then they'll all watch. Then, when we've finished, they'll telephone the police and complain. Anyway, what does it matter? Keep down and make them crane their necks.'

He did what she wanted him to as carefully as he could, holding himself a little aloof in order to concentrate, despite the worrying circumstances. Once, the clock on the mantel-piece started again, ticked for a few minutes, and stopped. Vibrations.

'You're mad,' he said to her. 'We both must be mad. This is Sunday, and I don't even know you.'

When they had finished, her face retained a curious vacant radiance. The long reddish hair made a sunburst on the fat brown arm of the sofa. She raised her hands and crossed them, so that her wrists covered her breasts. Smiling, she interlaced her fingers and went through the old children's jingle:

> There's the church
> There's the steeple.

Open the doors –
And there's all the people!

She flicked her fingers outwards in the final gesture of the tableau and then gazed at him, inscrutable, calmly bearing his weight. He shifted over to one elbow, and with his free hand played with a long auburn tress where it strayed over her shoulder and over the arm of the sofa.

'You must be mad,' he said again. 'All this is mad. I can't believe it's happening. I was on my way to get the Sunday papers, and this afternoon I have to go to work in a newspaper office. None of this makes any kind of sense.'

Another thought came to him. He gripped her bare shoulders, making her look at him.

'Where are all the people, anyway? The people in this house?'

The owl-like eyes never left his face.

'My father is at church.'

'At church? But it's after midday. That means he'll be back at any moment.'

She stared at him steadily. 'Yes. At any moment.'

She had scarcely uttered the words when the door of the room opened and a man stood in the dark aperture. No film editor could have timed the entrance more precisely, no actor could have picked up his cue more promptly.

What the newcomer saw was a young man, a stranger to him, sitting naked on the edge of the sofa, the small of his back pressed against the hip of a naked girl – a girl who met her father's horrified stare with total unconcern.

Douglas reached down and picked up his underpants and then held them in his lap, not wishing to add to his embarrassment, if that were possible, by trying to put them on. The old clock began to tick again.

The man in the doorway had indeed been to church. His neck was encircled by the narrow band of white, his chest covered by the black silk vest of a Church of Scotland minister. He was small and stout, with a pale face and protruding eyes, heavily circled. His bald head retained only a thin fringe of reddish hair, a faded reminder of his daughter.

He stood transfixed, his hand on the door handle, blinking his eyes as though struck a sudden and very violent blow. In his other hand he held a black church book. He must have come direct from the pulpit, from shaking hands with his congregation at the church door, from counting the collection with his elders. After what seemed a very long time he made an effort to speak, but before he could form any words there began a slow, inexorable twitching of the facial muscles. He came forward into the room and without a word subsided suddenly into one of the heavy old armchairs which made up the grossly upholstered three-piece suite. He put up a hand, plucked at the white collar, and closed his eyes.

Douglas took the opportunity to step into his underpants, pull on his other clothes, and find his tie where it had fallen over the back of the sofa. He made a clumsy knot.

The man in the chair was now being shaken by spasms. His limbs twitched, his face gradually turned an ugly blue.

'Good God,' said Douglas. 'He's having some sort of attack. Aren't you going to do anything? You'd better telephone at once.'

The sight of her caused him a new astonishment. She had not moved from where she lay, totally relaxed, on the huge brown sofa. She lay full length, casually regarding the inordinately high ceiling of the cavernous Georgian room.

Slowly and languorously she pulled down a rug from the back of the sofa and draped it across the top of her thighs and over one breast. On the other, the nipple showed rose pink against the fair skin.

'He's got a heart condition,' she said to the ceiling. 'He's had three attacks in two years. This is the fourth. The least little thing upsets him. It was bound to happen, sooner or later. It was only a matter of time.'

In a state of fearful indecision, Douglas approached the man in the chair. He had lolled over sideways. His head rested at a curiously unnatural angle, his mouth was slack and open, his lips and fingernails were blue. His eyes flickered, but seemed no longer to register what they saw. Douglas reached out a hand, unsure of how to loosen a minister's collar.

'Don't touch him,' the girl called sharply from the sofa. 'Unless you want to be involved. Why don't you just go? Go downstairs and straight across the hall and out into the street. The door has a Yale lock. Pull it shut behind you. It's Sunday, as you keep telling me. No one will see you, and even if they do, what does it matter? It's all quite natural, you know. In fact, "natural causes" is what they will call it.'

She suddenly got up, wrapping the rug round her, grimacing like someone who gets up on a cold night to close a banging door. She crossed to a drawer, pulled it open and took out a packet of cigarettes. She offered it to him.

'I only smoke cigars – now and again,' he mouthed stupidly.

'Too bad,' she said softly. 'No cigars in this house. No booze either. Only Christian charity, and, my God, all the bleakness that means.'

He stared at her.

'Now do you understand?'

'I think you ought to telephone,' he said, and looked vainly round the room for one. She took command again at once, in that way she had.

'Do you mind leaving now? I can handle everything. As

I said, it was only a matter of time. You can see that I'm quite glad it's happened. Now will you please just do as you're asked?'

Once more, Douglas looked helplessly round the room.

'Do make sure you haven't left anything.' Wide-eyed and quizzical, she blew a long stream of blue smoke at him, holding the rug round her with the other hand. That was her way of saying good-bye.

Avoiding the sight of the man in the chair he went out and closed the door carefully behind him. On the landing he listened, but no sound disturbed the silence of the unutterably gloomy house. The cupola at the top of the stair was as the sky might appear to a man at the bottom of a deep well.

Douglas tiptoed down the staircase and crossed the hall. He turned the Yale lock and drew open the heavy door, closing it behind him until the lock clicked. He took a deep breath of grey air, and mechanically set off eastwards along the great pillared block, towards home.

He met nobody. The churchgoers had retired indoors for their Sunday lunches. The Sunday calm had descended again over the New Town like a mortcloth.

Restless, hungry and incredulous he walked about his small attic flat for an hour, listening. On impulse he telephoned a friend who lived in Great Charlotte Street and asked him to look out of the window. The friend came back to say that there was only one car parked in the street – an ordinary black car, not a police car, not an ambulance.

Douglas lay on his bed, staring wide-eyed at the ceiling, until it was time to go to the office. For a while the rain came and slashed spitefully at the windows.

He worked his shift without retaining any impression of the news that passed beneath his sub-editor's pencil. When the copy boy dropped the first edition on his desk, he turned at once to the back page and scanned the columns of death notices – but of course it was far too soon for that. At half past eleven he left for home immediately, missing the usual visit to the canteen. He found that no note had been pushed through his letter box, and no CID men waited.

The next day he went at lunchtime to a small pub round the corner from Great Charlotte Street to see if anyone was talking about a happening in one of the big houses, but the discussion was, as usual, of the afternoon's racing, the seriousness of unemployment, the growing violence in the streets and how easily the perpetrators seemed to be getting away with it.

At his desk that night he scanned the death notices in the next day's paper with an eagerness which surprised the colleague sitting opposite.

One thing was certain: there had to be, sooner or later, a death notice for a Church of Scotland minister. That night he found it.

GIBSON. – Suddenly, at his home at 18, Great Charlotte Street, after Communion Service on Sunday, 28th January, The Rev. Walter Laing Gibson, for 31 years minister of Rodney Memorial Church, beloved husband of the late Elizabeth Rae Munro, and dear father of Caroline. Passed into the nearer presence of His Lord. Funeral service at the church on Thursday at 2 p.m., and thereafter privately to Dean Cemetery. No flowers or letters please.

Douglas became aware that the chief sub-editor was calling his name with increasing irritation. He rose and walked towards the top of the chaotic room, struggling to banish persistent recollections of the livid face, the starting eyes, the ringlets of Caroline's auburn hair on the fat arm of the sofa.

He performed the rest of the evening's work without remembering what it had been about. It was as if the sub-editing of item after item – the routine of assessment, correction, checking and cutting – had been taken over by some inner, more competent self. Thus the main part of him was left free to wonder and speculate.

So there were to be no letters and no flowers. Very unusual for a minister, staunch son of the Church. No doubt there would be a suitably large attendance at the funeral. Paeans of praise from the pulpit: a hardworking servant of the parish struck down in the midst of his harvest field . . . Caroline in black.

When the shift ended he walked home by a long round-about route – entering the New Town at its western edge and traversing all of its inscrutable streets, flanked by lights shining dimly behind closed curtains. He was unable to resist passing the house. It was, as expected of it, curtained and in total darkness. Natural causes, of course.

As the days went past, Douglas was unable to rid himself of a shrinking anticipation. The New Town being the social ghetto that it is, it was only a matter of time before he met her again. He therefore braced himself for a possible confrontation round every street corner, in every shop, even in the tiny bar where certain New Town residents met every evening, without necessarily speaking to each other.

After three weeks, and not even a distant glimpse of her, he began to wonder whether the whole episode had not been a hideous waking dream which had tricked him into involving all his senses. Only the death notice, concealed in his blotter at the office, prevented him from consigning Caroline to the realms of monstrous fantasy.

Then there came a Saturday morning, when he stood in a queue in the Pakistani shop, making the usual selection of green peppers and bananas. At first he was conscious of somebody at the head of the queue having amassed a prodigious quantity of groceries, and of the Pakistani taking a long time to note the prices.

Frowning at the delay and craning his neck, Douglas caught a glint of auburn hair, a sunburst set off by the cheap strip lighting attached to the grimy ceiling. As the Pakistani gathered her groceries and pushed them into her shopping bag, she turned to take the necessary money from her purse. She wore a black coat with a neat Astrakhan collar. The thin lips murmured something as the slender fingers pried for the smaller coins.

Caroline gave exactly the right change.

The Pakistani smiled at her back as she walked away from him, along the queue to the door.

Douglas kept his eyes steadily on her face as she came towards him. For perhaps a second, a long second, her eyes met his. Then she was level with him, past him, and gone. Her firm footsteps rang on the stone steps up to the street.

Douglas, with a tight, fixed smile, waited to pay for his groceries. How plain she had made it to the people in the shop that, with or without her contact lenses, she did not know any of them.

3

PATSY THOMSON

THERESA, SHUGGIE AND THE TANNIES

GLASGOW'S BOTANICAL GARDENS are quiet. Sunday afternoon and winter too.

Still it's busy enough inside the Kibble Palace – cosy here amongst the palms, fruit trees and statuary – a Victorian legacy to the frail and foreign flotsam of the West End. One old woman, threadbare and douce, sits at the far end of a bench from two gently muttering Sikhs, and pitches bread-crumbs to the sparrows. Pampered tropical sparrows these – hard to imagine them ever trying to fly out through the open skylights, way up in the fretted glass dome. They've got it made – light, heat, foliage, food. Outside, feathered proles are shivering and narking in Glasgow January – man, if they only knew – one quick sprint to the top of the Kibble and instant sparrow Nirvana.

A short way from the Palace stand the hot-houses – wet, warm, magnificent. People ponderously remove overcoats and study labels – they've come to smell hyacinths and ogle obscene orchids.

Outside and up the hill by the flag-pole there's a children's playspace with mini-chute, rocking-boat and caged-in swings. Parents grumble at kids – uptight middle-class parents who are anxious that Sophie, Jake or Benjamin should stock up on moral fibre by sliding down the chute unaided. Glasgow's working-class mothers and fathers sit snug in single-ends and follow the ITV Seven while their weans run free.

Nobody croons or clucks over Theresa and Shuggie as they wander the Tannies, self-sufficient and untrammelled. Theresa is seven, Shuggie four or so. Both look scraggy and shilpit in sandshoes, jeans, shirts and frayed cardigans. They're out and no hope of being let back in before five thirty.

They sidle into the Kibble Palace, pockets stuffed with pebbles. What should they go for first, goldfish or sparrows? The fish sensing trouble, cluster at the bottom of the orna-mental pond. Theresa squats by the stone rim, prepared to wait. Shuggie squints at the water. Soon a fat albino fish, too bored or too moronic to stay in the central depths, circles the pool inches below the surface. Shuggie nudges Theresa who is already taking aim, then dips into his arsenal. 'Let the bastard have it' – on Theresa's whispered command gravel pelts the water. A startled white fish dives. Convinced of a kill the children move off. They tour the Palace on the look-out for senile sparrows to stone, but senility seems the prerogative of the human occupants. Shuggie doesn't much like passing the old stale men and women, but Theresa knows where there's a dirty statue. A white marble nude looks chastely ahead while two kids snicker and stretch up to touch her nipples.

They will have to hurry to reach the hot-houses before they close. A dash along a tarmac path, then there's a heavy wooden door to push and they've made it. They slope past the attendant when he's not looking ('children not admitted unless accompanied by a responsible adult') into the desert house where daemonic cacti loom – it's a point of honour to test the spikes. Theresa once cut herself on the pampas grass. The two kids advance on the equatorial house. Date trees, lianas and steam everywhere. Even Theresa is slightly awed. They keep to the paving till they can see the ironwork staircase. It winds its surrealist way right to the roof of the glass-house and is gated and padlocked. Theresa clambers over, hauling Shuggie after her. Up and around the glossy white steps they climb. When they are on a level with the palm fronds they lean over to grab them, savouring the rich damp growth. Down and around and off again. The big tank with the lilypads receives the last of the pebbles and then the children start on the return route. They run through the varying temperatures, leaving doors open that ought to be shut, weaving their way from continent to continent. They do stop once, though, to gawp at the glassed-in horror of the carnivorous plants. Venus fly-traps play up to the audience – tiny insects visibly caught in sticky maws. Theresa and Shuggie move on and out.

Theresa runs up the broad empty walk to the flag-pole. Sandshoes belt the tarmac and navy cardigans flap as Shuggie does his best to give her some kind of race. They leave the path and skilfully dodging dog-shit pound over the grass to the flag-pole. It's tall, thick, guyed-up with strong wires. Shuggie leans his head back, straining to catch sight of the very top. There's a fish-shaped weather-vane way up there. At last Shuggie spots the dingy zeppelin – honour satisfied he uncricks his neck. Theresa says they fly a flag once a year – Queen's birthday or something daft like that. Glaswegians are not reared on a diet of colour and pageantry, so Shuggie accepts the bare, mean, flag-less pole. They play on the guy-wires, dangling their weight from their hands and sticking out their tongues, doing an ape-man bit. It's kind of tiring.

Down they drop and away to the playpark. A few parents and children are still there. Shuggie rummels up the chute queue. Little girls whimper and small boys keen, as he shoves his neighbours on the steps. Sodden sandshoes smear well-tended clothes. He's at the top now, turns casually and slides down – headfirst, backwards. Looks of disgust and admiration follow him over to the rocking-boat. Theresa sits waiting perched at one end. Shuggie takes up position at the other and they set to work. The boat begins to sway. It's long, and soon rocks alarmingly as Theresa and Shuggie crouch like jockeys urging on rival horses. They lean and press and shout and terrify. Unwary toddlers are scooped out of range of the bucking leviathan. Vague mutters of 'Time for tea now darlings' are met with unusually prompt responses and adults and offspring evaporate from the scene, amour-propre shattered. Having scared off the opposition, Theresa and Shuggie bask in their territorial supremacy. Time for a swing. They stand on the plastic seats, grip the cold chains and ripple their bodies slowly backwards and forwards.

It must be getting near five now. They swing on until the University clock booms out the hour. Then they are off over the grassy hilltop.

Diagonal paths tack their way sedately to the River Kelvin far below, but Shuggie and Theresa crash straight down and down. It's a steep tricky descent and they are winded and exhilarated when they reach the bottom. They cross the solid sandstone bridge, pausing to spit over the balustrade. Some river, the Kelvin – littered, brown and smelly any day of the year. Theresa says a boy up their way fell in and died of the poison. Shuggie believes her.

Once they are over the bridge it's a daunder up the hill to the gap in the railings. They prise each other through, scorning the open gate some hundred yards out of their way. Theresa and Shuggie scuff their sandshoes on the road, heading for ham and eggs and home – three up, right hand side.

4

DEIRDRE CHAPMAN

INTO EUROPE

'SHARL...'

'Oui p'tit chou?'

'Arrêtez immedibloodyatement.'

'Patience my dove. It is but two hours less a quarter.'

'You keep going on and on. I've seen at least six places and you keep going on.'

The Clarks were one and a half days from Boulogne, heading into the interior. Their Scottish-built Imp said 'Écosse' on the back and 'It's Scotland's Oil' on the windscreen. As it juddered past a dawdling Mercedes, their sleeping sons Callum and Rory collided on the back seat and sat up blinking in a flurry of crumbs and Kleenex.

'Is this still France, Daddy?'

Callum was wrestling with the concept of roads. It seemed an endless strip of tarmac circled the world carrying through traffic. To get to proper places like the Eiffel Tower or the Leaning Tower of Pisa you had to get off the road and in behind those hedges. He wished they'd get off the road.

'When are we having our picnic?'

He'd had nothing for breakfast but a bent roll that tasted more like a cookie.

'Say it louder, darling. Daddy's a bit blocked. Things aren't getting through. You too, Rory. All together now. "WHEN ARE WE HAVING OUR PICNIC, DADDY?"

Very good. Now naughty Daddy will have to stop going on and on.'

Charles, who liked going on and on, felt pressured to invent a destination.

'I'm looking for a river,' he said. 'Déjeuner sur l'herbe. Près de l'eau. Sous les arbres.'

'Avec les midges.'

'Bugger the midges. I'm looking for a river to cool the wine.'

And, now that he'd said it, it seemed the idea had been germinating pleasantly in his head all morning.

Spotting a likely sign he spun the wheel and the Imp nipped under the nose of a family Peugeot and scuttled off down a slip road. Behind them the Peugeot howled with outrage and the Mercedes flowed past unchecked. 'Curses,' said Charles, who'd worked for half an hour to overtake it.

They were in a narrow twisting road dropping away from the route nationale between shaggy verges and straggling cottages. Hens scattered round a blind bend and a man in faded denim leant on a spade and watched them go.

'Which river are we looking for, Daddy: the River Clyde, the River Nile, the River Rhine . . . ?'

'The River Allier. What did that sign say, Helen?'

'Pont de something. Keep going. I bet it's a foul trickle full of old prams.'

'The route map says "A straight and level road through agricultural country becoming sinuous through the more picturesque scenery beside the broad River Allier".'

'What's sinuous, Daddy?'

'Twisty, Callum. But not *just* twisty. There's a suggestion of movement too. You wouldn't call a liquorice stick sinuous, for example. It's twisty, all right, but it's twisty in a rigid sort of way.'

'Daddy . . .'

'Quiet, Callum. When you ask a question you listen to the answer. Let's see if we can think of anything else that's sinuous. We've got a road and a river. What else moves in a twisty sort of way?'

'A snake.'

'Well done, Mummy. Mummy says a snake.'

'Daddy . . .'

'I've told you not to interrupt. Now we've got a snake. A snake stationary is straight. But when it moves it doesn't go along all in one piece like you do or Spotty does . . .'

'I want Spotty. I *want* Spotty.'

'Spotty's very happy with the nice lady in the kennels, Rory, playing with all the other doggies.'

'Daddy . . .'

'I wish you'd be quiet, Callum. I can't concentrate on driving and explain things to you and have you interrupting all the time. Now a snake is sinuous when it moves because . . .'

'But Daddy we've passed the river.'

'Where?'

'Back where the trees were.'

'Nonsense.'

'I can see something glinting through the trees, Charles.'

'Well I wish you'd said so before. I can't do all the driving *and* the navigating *and* watch out for bloody rivers.'

The road had carried them into a skeletal village, two sides of a funnel, a short funnel.

'God, what a nowhere place,' Helen said.

The church was big enough, though, to cast a black shadow outside the café. In the shadow the population sat.

Callum wondered where all the children were. Maybe they had died, in the heat. And the mummies, too, where were the mummies? The busy mummies in their light coats and red clacky shoes pushing their shopping trolleys, racing one another to the shops, looking in the windows, looking at nothing but stacks of canned peaches and tea bags with 2p off. Where were the windows? Where were the shops?

Something dreadful had happened here. Only the grannies were left.

Charles pulled up at the café and took off his dark glasses so they could see his eyes were friendly.

He shouted, 'Pardonnez moi, où est la rivière?'

The population went into a huddle. Charles revved tetchily. 'You'd think they'd remember where their bloody river was.'

'It's your accent, darling. They're interpreting.'

A small fierce man, bristly, with little eyes like a wild boar, approached the car. His wrinkled fingers were indented with gold rings. All the grannies watched him. One of them was knitting without looking at the pins. Callum thought maybe he was going to shoot them.

'Anglais?'

'Écossais.'

'Huh. The river is là-bas. You go bac bac bac. Always bac.'

'Merci.'

'M'sieur.'

'You see,' Charles said, reversing, 'it always does the trick. As soon as they know you're Scottish they can't do enough to help you.'

Rory said nothing. In a dark doorway he'd seen a witch, all in black, leaning on a broomstick.

Back amongst the trees they turned left over a broad stone bridge, and pulled up in a half-cleared bramble patch. Charles killed the engine. The radiator boiled painfully to a standstill. In the silence the river could be heard, moving.

'The car,' said Helen, 'is an international zone. When the engine stops we're suddenly in France.'

Charles unsprang the safety catch and the children, released, tumbled out and slithered off into the undergrowth to catch up on the day.

Helen peeled her thighs off the hot Rexine and hobbled out into France. Charles was throwing the picnic things out of the boot into the long grass. Grasshoppers started up angrily where they fell.

'Écoutez les fourmis!'

'Don't be ridiculous, Helen, ants don't make a noise.'

'Fourmi is grasshopper. We had a poem at school, "La Cigale et le Fourmi." The ant and the grasshopper.'

'The grasshopper and the ant.'

'Are you sure?'

'Sure I'm sure. Fourmi is ant. Formic acid is derived from it.'

'From an ant? What do they use it for?'

'How do I know what they use it for? It's from an ant, though.'

'You'd wonder how they ever discovered it, wouldn't you?'

With holdall, basket and carrier the Clarks advanced into the undergrowth. Helen's sling-backs scooped up mud like a bottom-grubbing duck and fed it up between her toes. Cold leaves stroked her bare arms and thorns picked at her dress.

When they came out into the sunshine they were in a fairy ring of cropped grass, open at one side to the river. Behind them the bushes closed up against the shoulder of the bridge. Their eyes scaled its height to the parapet, toppling against a moving sky, and, under the pale curve of its armpit, trembling water patterns.

Helen spread her arms prettily to embrace it all, their bridge, their river, their clearing.

'It's all ours, not a soul in sight.'

'I told you I'd fix it, didn't I?'

They kissed then, still holding the baskets, in a spotlight of slanting sun. Like a pair of Peynet lovers, Helen thought. Then Charles went off with the boys to relieve himself and cool the wine in the river.

Helen spread the red checked cloth in full sunlight where the grass was flattened. The French were odd the way they hugged the shade.

The pâté was rather warm and bitty, the Camembert moulded to the shape of the wine bottle. And the plastic plates were hot and smelly with echoes of past picnics. She picked some broad leaves and used them as doylies. She hoped they weren't poisonous. She felt quite paysanne and provident.

When Charles came back she was pouring liquid butter out of a hot plastic box into a nettle patch. He picked up the long loaf and began to slice it in his hand in the French way. When he nicked his finger he said 'sacré bleu' and wrapped it in a red paper napkin. It was so quiet they could hear the crumbs drop.

Helen wriggled out of the top half of her dress and sat there in her bra. 'Let's buy a cottage in France, darling.'

'What's wrong with the Highlands?'

'Too farouche. Nothing but sliced bread and you can't take children in the pubs. No. France is for me. I'll bottle fruit and preserve goose and you'll wear a funny straw hat and hoe the field. And we'll keep a goat called Clothilde.'

'What field?'

'We'll need a field for you to play with. Like those peasants in the north. All in funny hats and hoeing. With their children too. It looked fun. We could cash in an insurance policy or sell our Scotbits. I bet you can buy a cottage here for peanuts.'

With wild warcries the children came bounding out of the

nettles, leaving footprints of molten butter all over the tablecloth.

Charles slapped Callum and Helen smacked Rory, quite hard, out of fright, and he sat down suddenly on the tablecloth and howled.

'All right, Rory, all right, darling. Mummy didn't hurt you. Mummy has to smack Rory sometimes so that he'll look where he's going the next time.'

'Shut up, Helen, and find some bloody dockens. Can't you see the child's covered with nettle stings.'

Charles snatched all Helen's doylies off the plates and scrubbed at Rory's legs, green spinachy lumps among the red blotches. Callum was suddenly sick in a bush.

'I'm car sick, Mummy.'

'Nonsense, darling, no one's car sick after the car has stopped.'

'I am, Mummy.'

Helen picked the pâté and the Camembert out of the grass and wiped them off with a Kleenex. Charles took it from her and wiped Rory's eyes.

'Now watch you don't go near that bush. I'll put a newspaper over it just in case. And stay out of nettles in future.'

'What's nettles, Daddy?'

'Good God, Helen, haven't you even taught the child what a nettle looks like?'

They ate, then, in four degrees of silence. Helen fantasised a French lover smouldering beside her in the grass, eating a peach. What a pity he was such a noisy eater.

Rory was an ant, hacking his way through the impenetrable grass, watching out for the dread sinuous caterpillar.

Callum swam powerfully across the river to rescue a dog, no, two dogs, cheered on by the staff and pupils of Greenside Primary.

Charles had a Citroen up there in the clearing and a mistress in Neuilly. The responsibility of it cast a tiny grey cloud over his happiness.

All the time little grass creatures came and bit their legs, and the river passed quietly towards a meaningless sea.

The silence cracked suddenly like an empty glass. Particles of sound fell down to them from the bridge and as the bushes began to shake and crackle Rory sat bolt upright and proclaimed in a sonorous voice, 'Here Comes The Sinuous Snake.'

But it was only some children. Callum was glad they weren't dead, though they didn't look like real boys either. They were all dressed in blue, the colour of deckchairs that get left out all summer in the sun and rain. And their arms and legs were greyish-brown.

Helen thought they were beautiful. Their heads were neat and woolly like field mice. Her fingertips tingled with wanting to pat them. Only then she remembered about her dress and tried to get back into it.

The leader nodded. 'M'sieur dame.' He stepped off the path into the long wet grass, making a display of it, taking a wide berth round them, and emerging back onto the path with his espadrilles sodden.

'M'sieur dame.'

'M'sieur dame.'

'M'sieur dame.'

'What did they *say*, Daddy? What did it mean?'

'Mr and Mrs. French children are very polite.'

'So are we,' said Callum sullenly.

'So am I,' said Rory.

'You told me,' said Callum, 'it was rude to call people mister or missus.'

'It's different in France.'

'M'sieur dame.'

44

'M'sieur dame.'

'It's like the Champs Elysées in rush hour.'

'You've set the table right in the middle of their bloody thoroughfare.'

'How would you like to be a little French boy, Callum, and come here every day?'

'I'm a Scottish boy,' said Callum.

'Me Scottish boy too,' said Rory.

How pink they are, Helen thought, how pink and squat and stocky. They'll never tan with that carroty hair. They'll just go to freckles.

Charles said, 'When you're big boys Mummy and Daddy will send you to stay with a French family. And then we'll have their boys to stay with us.'

And what will their boys think of that, Helen wondered. Our boys are children. French boys are men, waiting for their turn.

'You see, Cally, the French people and the Scottish people are special friends. They used to get together to fight the English people.'

They would look much better if they didn't wear those awful green tee shirts, Helen thought. Green is such an industrial colour. Northern and industrial. They wear them because of Celtic and then everyone thinks we're Catholics. Of course it's all right being a Catholic if you're a French Catholic. It's different in France.

'Do the boys know we're friends?'

'How do you mean?'

'Do they know we're Scottish boys?'

'We-ell, probably not. You see the Scottish people and the English people speak the same language. Of course when you learn to speak French they'll know you're Scottish because Scottish people speak French much better than English people. If Mummy hadn't packed so many clothes for herself we'd have brought your kilts and then everybody would have known you were Scottish boys.'

'If you learn to speak French very well and practise your manners, some day they might even think you're French boys.'

'My juice is sour,' said Callum, truculent with his failure to be French.

'Nonsense, it's lovely French apple juice.'

'My duce sour too.'

'Don't be a copy-cat, Rory.'

'Mummy's duce sour?'

'Mummy isn't drinking apple juice, Mummy's drinking grape juice. Special grape juice for grown-ups. They've done special things to it. Like they do special things to apple juice to make – here, Rory, let Mummy taste your juice. Good God. It's cider. It had an apple on the label. I didn't think . . . no, Rory, you mustn't drink any more. It's not little boys' apple juice. I don't care if you *are* thirsty, give me that cup . . . you little brat!'

Helen stood up, dripping. Rory hurled the cup at her and lay back, roaring. One Startrite sandal flew off and landed on the pâté. Callum moved cautiously out of range of the flailing feet and began to giggle. He giggled till his chest ached, rolling in the grass, cool and tickly on his tingling face, laughing his defiance at them, hearing his own voice laughing and laughing back at it.

'They're stoned out of their minds,' said Charles.

'French children drink wine from the cradle,' said Helen.

It was Charles who picked them up and straightened their tee shirts and took them off to sober up in the river.

Helen lay back to sunbathe with her dress top off. Resting her eyes amongst the murky underpinnings of the bridge she saw a movement. A pair of eyes met hers. A boy was sitting astride a girder directly overhead.

Helen shrugged back into her dress and glared. The boy shifted position and a piece of grit fell into her eye. She sat up angrily. A Peeping French bloody Tom and not even out of short pants. And she had to get behind a bush soon or burst.

On the fringe of the bushes she looked up again. He was still there. Casually she began to pick sprays of blossom, arranging them fussily as if she had all the time in the world. Her dress kept snagging on the thorns as she worked her way farther into the bushes. When she seemed to be well screened she looked back. The boy was still on her skyline, smiling now.

Furiously tearing off any branch that would come away she hacked on into the thicket. Every time she looked back the eyes were following her, obscene adult's eyes in a child's face.

Charles and his sons laid their six sensible brown sandals in a row and stood hand and hand in the shallows, watching their white feet turn scarlet.

The French boys were on a concrete island where the bridge touched down in midstream. Seeing them, they began to display to the foreigners, pushing one another off and swimming splashily back to the island.

'They can swim, Daddy,' Callum whispered, 'swim proply. I can just pretend.'

'Let's show them a thing or two, shall we?'

Charles picked up a flat stone.

'Watch this.'

His arm described a perfect curve and at just the right second his fingers opened and flicked. Slap slap plop.

The French boys stopped splashing and watched. Rory jumped up and down and tugged at his father's shirt tail.

'Me try, Daddy, me try.'

Charles slotted a stone into Rory's small palm and worked his arm from behind. Slap plop.

'Again, Daddy.'

'No, it's Cally's turn.' Plop. 'Hard luck, Cally, try again.' Plop. 'Look, Daddy will show you how.'

This stone was a beaut. Five times it skimmed and hopped before it disappeared. Rory was wild with pride and the French boys gave up their game and started swimming towards them.

'Me try again Daddy.'

Rory snatched the stone from his father's hand, a thin sharp-edged one like a flake of slate, and flung it wildly, straight at the oncoming boys.

Charles closed his eyes. He wondered if French boys were too God-fearing to swear. Hopelessly he started batting around in his brain for the French for 'sorry'. 'Dommage' – that rang a bell.'

'Quel dommage!' he said out loud.

As the leading swimmer stepped out on to the bank, bleeding profusely from the forehead, he realized he had said 'What a pity.' A mad snigger escaped him. He looked at the boy helplessly and the boy looked at him. Between them incomprehension settled like slow sediment.

It was Rory who broke silence. Staring at the boy and trembling all over with excitement, he pointed at the blood snaking from drop to drop down his wet cheek.

'Look look,' he shouted. 'Sin' he yelled, 'sin you', he was ecstatic, 'sin youus!'

Slowly the boy bent to pick up a stone. Charles noted miserably that it wasn't flat.

In desperation Helen had dropped to her knees and crawled under a dense bush. Cider had cemented her skirt to her legs and bits of tree jabbed her shoulders and fell down her neck as she struggled.

When she crawled out again the boy was still there. She should have thrown something at him, words even. But she stood there, weakly, pinned by the skirt, the hair, the buttonhole.

From the direction of the river a child's scream came to her. Then she saw the top of Charles's head moving quickly above the bushes.

It seemed to her they would pass her by, get into the car, and drive off while she struggled here alone in the thorns beneath the laughing boy. Pushing, tearing and calling she charged through the bushes and fell out bloodstained at Charles's bare feet.

Rory was in his arms, blood trickling from a cut across his cheekbone. Callum came behind with all the sandals.

'For Christ's sake what *happened*?'

'He was stoned.'

'You mean it was an accident?'

'No accident.'

'But surely . . . well if it wasn't an accident hadn't you better do something about it?'

Charles looked back. Boys stood where the path met the river, waiting. Helen looked up. A solitary boy sat on a girder, watching.

The Clarks gathered the plastic plates into their tartan holdall and collected the rubbish carefully into a polythene peddle-bin liner. Turning their backs on the river they tramped back through the bushes to the car.

Rory sat on Helen's knee and Callum squeezed on to the front seat beside her so that it was hard for Charles to engage second gear.

As the car turned back across the bridge towards the main road he said 'Daddy . . .'

'Yes, Callum?'

'We should have weared our kilts.'

5

ELSPETH DAVIE

THE COLOUR

Mr Garrad had rung rather late in the day – some time after tea when the disorder had shown itself. But it wasn't as late as all that. And anyway they'd had it in writing that, in an emergency, someone could come right away. It was urgent all right – not something to be cured at home by a bit of tinkering and on-the-spot treatment. It was not the first time it had happened either. Garrad looked pained when he came back from the phone. His wife sat on the sofa nursing a pillow for comfort. She knew instinctively that it would be a comfortless evening. The son and daughter had emerged from their bedrooms and hung limply on the banisters to hear the diagnosis.

'They will come this evening,' said Garrad, sitting down at the other end of the sofa. 'And they will do something about it, if possible.' That was the devil of it – the 'if possible' which sounded the dirge on hope. How many 'if possibles' had these two not heard – and yet weren't used to it yet.

'If possible?' muttered his wife, as though testing out a foreign phrase in her mouth.

'That's it. I'm giving you their word for word.' They sat in silence.

'What will you do then? Will you go out?' said the wife after a bit.

'I'll wait till they come. *If* they come. Then I'll go out.'

They waited fifty minutes until, as by a miracle, the two young men turned up. The family watched them as they knelt and tested and talked together. Nothing came of it. All the others could see was the odd red streak that made the heart jump till they saw it was only the reflection of the bus-stop sign on the other side of the street. The men answered Garrad's questions. They were very young. But it wasn't their age that bothered him. It was their politeness, their gentleness. They had the cheerful gentleness of stretcher-bearers on a serious case as they lifted the set in their arms and carried it out. This same pair had actually put in the colour. Now, for the second time, they were taking it away. 'How long this time?' Garrad asked as they went past him, carefully manoeuvring it round the corner of the passage and shielding it fom the sharp edge of the hall table. They shook their heads and smiled. He watched them go through the front door, careful not to jolt or trip. He watched the colour being carried farther and farther away until it finally disappeared into the waiting van.

'Well, that's that!' he cried coming back, falsely cheerful, into the living-room.

'Nobody minds a couple of nights without,' said his wife. 'But there's Friday. It's Friday I'm thinking about.'

'And Sunday' he added. On Friday there was a thriller serial two episodes from the end. There was also a cookery demonstration which they all watched hungrily week by week, never mind whether they'd had their meal or not. They were hungry for the colour of this food – the familiar yellow yolks of eggs being broken into scarlet bowls, white cream poured into chocolate sauce, and all stirred with a blue spoon. In the background tomatoes were piled against black aubergines, polished like ebony – on the side, platters of apples, grapes and oranges. Now and then the demonstrator would wipe her hands on an apron striped green and

blue. Garrad's wife was a good cook herself. She used milk
and eggs. She could have got a scarlet bowl if she'd wanted
it. She'd have been the first to admit her milk was whiter,
the eggs yellower than the screen ones. But that was not the
point. Where was the comfort in it? For Garrad, who liked
the country, there was a regular Sunday series of different
landscapes filmed hour by hour from dawn to moonrise,
showing the changing colours of sky, field and river
throughout one day. The colour wasn't bad in Garrad's
estimation. It was as real as you could get unless you
actually had the thing itself behind you in the window.
They'd done a good job on colour and the chances were it
would get better as time went on.

'You're going out then?' said his wife.

'Might as well.' He stepped out into the street, into a
warm autumn evening. His own street was made up of small
modern houses with long gardens, well-known in the
district for their new-planted trees. Most people were tend-
ing a sapling. Garrad was proud of this himself but this
evening he had no eyes for the spindly branches beside him.
In spite of himself he kept looking up at the TV aerials
growing overhead, frail-looking, yet tough enough to with-
stand the most ferocious blast. Not one house without these
magic roof-twigs. All the same he was the only man for a
long way round these parts who had colour. The first man.
A kind of Adam of the new vision. Very soon – perhaps in a
year or so – possibly in a few months, they'd all have it. But
he was the first. He strode along quickly at first, then
gradually more and more slowly as the first fury of his frust-
ration spent itself. He was able to smile at the few persons
he knew who were sitting at windows or working in their
gardens along the street. At one or two he stopped. A married couple he knew rather better than the rest were out
staring at a bed of roses and Garrad stopped and stared too.

'You're out early,' the man remarked, stepping across the bed towards him.

'Yes. Good to get a breath of air after the office.'

'And the wife?'

'Fine. Or not bad is more like it. She gets easily put out, thrown off her stroke . . .'

'But she's well?'

'She worries.'

'Like the rest of us. And yourself?'

'All right. Rather dull, as you see.'

'Sorry to hear your wife has worries,' said the woman. 'Not serious ones I hope.'

'Nothing much. It's the colour trouble again. Have you thought about colour yourself?'

They immediately stripped themselves of all frivolity, let go of the roses. 'Colour? I may say we read and listen to everything that's being said on that particular issue,' the man said. 'I think you know my views on the colour question.'

'It wasn't that though. It's colour TV I'm talking about.'

'Oh I see. No I've no views on that, I'm afraid. Not yet. Haven't got the money to have any views on that at the moment. Now, this colour question. As I said before – I think you know my views on that.'

'Certainly I know them. I share them.'

'I hope you do.'

'That's a queer way to put it, and not particularly complimentary to Mr Garrad here,' said his wife coming nearer. 'You're implying he may have prejudices of one kind or another or that he's afraid to come out with them.'

'What utter nonsense! But there *is* a queer thing. Here we are all airing our views about colour, with lowered voices. Some day, looking back, the world will think it's unbelievably ludicrous. We'll be all colours and thankful to be. It'll be a disgrace to be pure white, pure black, brown or yellow. That's how it'll be in the world to come.'

'In a future world you mean,' said his wife.

'The same.'

'Because "world to come" usually means "next life". Which is a very different matter.'

'I have no views about a next life, none whatever. Except there's said to be no marriage or giving in marriage and that's all that interests me.'

'So you can see where your colour views get us,' said his wife to Garrad. 'I hope your wife doesn't get what I have to put up with. And by the way, what about a bunch of roses to take back?'

'Lovely,' said Garrad quickly. 'Lovely. But I'll get them on the way back if it's all the same . . .'

He moved on past other gardens competing in brightness and neatness, past doors painted blue, white and green, and down to the busy corner and round it and on towards the part which grew more and more congested near the crossing of main roads but where, miraculously, on clear days, in a closed-in wedge between a pub and a church, you could just see the blue line of distant sea. When he was a young man Garrad had cherished this almost invisible wedge of the town. There was some fractional romance about it which he occasionally remembered nowadays when he was struggling through rush-hour crowds or waiting in longer or longer queues. There was sometimes a pin-pointing of clouds over this sea, now and then the fleck of a ship. Sometimes it was no more than the narrow dazzle of light between black brick. He seldom looked for it now. When he looked he seldom saw it. Twenty more years of traffic had nearly obscured it. A smart addition to the church and a new signboard on the pub had pared it to an even smaller piece of sea and sky. He went farther and farther into the centre and slowly out again on the other side where most of the town's public buildings stood – banks, town hall, libraries and Technical College – all with a sizeable bit of green in front. He came to the main modern school with its huge glass frontage where you could look right into empty class-rooms and corridors and see flowers blazing along the sills, and maps, mobiles, posters on the opposite walls. A late janitor strolled up to the gates as he went past.

'Ah . . . the young devils . . . they're in luck, aren't they?' Garrad said. 'They're never done looking. They can see the whole world go past as they do their sums. When I think how we had to fix our eyes on a 2 by 3 block of blackboard! There wasn't anywhere else to look. What wouldn't we have given to see all this!'

'But would you say it was a *good* thing?' said the janitor, leaning his elbow on a spike of railing.

'I was just coming to that. Is it?' said Garrad. 'Does it help them concentrate? Does it even help them choose what things to look at out of all the stuff going past the window? Does it make them selective? S-e-l-e-c-t-i-v-e.' Garrad rolled and relished the word on his tongue. The janitor took his elbow off the spike for a moment. 'And these are going too.'

'What's that?'

'The spikes are going.'

'Well that's good I suppose. No spikes, eh? All this and spikeless too. Makes you wonder how we came through at all at their age.' He walked on gravely, passing one or two acquaintances on his way. He made this distinction with middle age. Real friends got fewer and fewer while acquaint-ances grew and multiplied. These days he used the word 'real' a lot. Real. He hung on grimly to reality like an acrobat with a metal plug between the teeth, hanging over a void. Real friends, real food, real entertainment, real service, real flavour, real bread, real leather, real hair, real meat, real money, real women. They were all whizzing away from him. Real colour. It was not yet added to his list.

It was cooler now and the street quieter. At another crossing of streets a miniature market was packing up its stalls. Men, untying aprons blotched with juice, were getting ready to heave up piles of empty crates on to lorries or into their shops behind, while round about a few left-over baskets of battered fruit were being fingered by latecomers. A few stalls were still intact. One was slung round like an Arabian tent with purple and crimson cloth, overhung with long red and blue nylon dresses with flowered sashes. Rows of boots, dangling from their laces round the top of the stall, kicked half-heartedly in the breeze as though engaged in some mild, disembodied game of football.

A couple who were hurrying past stopped suddenly beside Garrad. They were coming from their shop where, over a long time-span of changing fashions, every single object there had changed from junk to antique and back to junk again. They kept their spirits up.

'Hullo, Mr Garrad. Very thoughtful you look. Are you contemplating the skating boots up there or what?' said the husband.

'Well I might yet. Right now I'm only out for a stroll.'

'Good. But don't forget to be back for seven, will you?'

'Seven. What's that?'

'What's seven! Don't tell me you were thinking of giving a miss to the last of the Great Gardens?'

'I've no choice. It's broken down on us.' Garrad told the tale again. Of how colour was brought and taken back, and brought and taken back again. He didn't fuss – simply told it with a wry smile while they exclaimed in sympathy. But they were still leaning at a steep angle towards home. 'So we'd have been better to stay with black and white for a while,' Garrad went on. 'That way we'd never have known what we were missing.'

'Do you think so?' Their faces lost a little sympathy. They had no colour. Garrad knew he had been tactless.

'It's just,' he said, 'that it doesn't take long to get used to colour.'

'I suppose so,' said the wife. 'Do you find it true?'

'True?'

'Yes, I believe it varies a lot. Some say they'll never get it true to life.'

'Well it's different of course.'

'They're never going to get it absolutely true. That's what I heard.'

'I wouldn't say never. Depends what you mean by true. It's going to get better and better.'

'Does anything?' said the man. 'I'm afraid I'm a pessimist. And I'm rather odd about colour. I don't believe I'd like it unless it was absolutely true. I suppose you could call me a bit of an artist. Isn't that so, Lena?'

'It is,' said his wife without enthusiasm.

'Not in anything I do, of course. But in how I look at things.'

'And everyone sees things differently,' said Garrad.

'But not as differently as colour TV sees them.' There was some severity in the man's tone. Garrad said nothing. He pretended to look around him at the world. He didn't tell this couple that he'd come to like the blue-tinged eggs, the etherialised pink of TV flesh. He had half a mind to confess, if they'd been in listening mood, that he found the world painfully hard-edged these days, almost too real, too steadily bright for comfort.

'And anyway,' the husband was saying, 'do I want it all in colour? Why not save something I can discover for myself?'

'Such as . . . ?' his wife asked.

'Well . . . all those exotic flowers and shrubs, if you like, on the Himalayan foothills.'

'You've left that pretty late,' she said. 'I don't think you're going to make it. And anyway I'm not worrying what *you* might or might not discover. What about invalids who can't get around at all? Don't you want them to have the benefit of seeing the world in colour?'

'Listen! It's the first time she's mentioned invalids and TV. The thing's a ruse to make out I'm bone selfish. And talking of invalids, I may say it's operations she'll go for if ever we get the colour. I mean the open heart and the bisected brain are going to be quite something, don't you agree?' They moved swiftly on their way towards home.

Garrad remained looking around him for a while, then wandered slowly back the way he'd come. Colour was beginning to go out of the streets and into the sky. Alleys, archways, back-courts were all a deeper grey, but the upper air was glowing. The open heart. He repeated it to himself. Now there was a phrase – a suggestive phrase meaning anything you cared to make it. It had a life apart from the operating-table. And there were some more prone to speak of hearts than others. Open hearts or broken hearts, warm hearts or cold ones – such words were easy for some people. But not to him. He never mentioned this heart to anyone, not even to himself. Yet it was real all right. In the world where he longed to keep a grip on all real things – heart still had meaning. He slowed down. His heart was beating strongly as it had done for the last sixty years, as it would do for the next – how many more? 'Well, I'm not so crazy about a long life,' he had murmured out loud. In the door-way of his shop near closing-time, James Byers heard him, heard the murmur 'not so crazy' and murmured very softly in reply:

'Now who would ever call *you* crazy, Mr Garrad?'

Garrad stopped abruptly, turned to the doorway and saw the spread of the evening newspaper, dark with disaster, and above it Byers' impassive face with its spectacled, secretive eyes looking at him. The shop had no need of billboards. Here, morning and evening in the doorway, Byers spread and read the paper. Passers-by read snippets hungrily and went in for more.

'I said I'm not all that crazy about a long life,' said Garrad. 'Look at old Peterson now, fumigated and isolated in his high-class nursing-home. I dread what I'll become. And in his own home – there was my father. Such a misery to himself and everyone else, poor man, from his eighty-eighth to his ninety-first, that his funeral went like a regular jamboree. The surprise was there was no cavorting and bawling.'

'You might be interested in a longer life when you come to it.'

'I doubt that. Ask me if you're still around.'

'I'll do that. This isn't your usual time for walking, Garrad – on a Wednesday evening.'

'It's not. I'm running from a sort of hole in our house.'

'A plumbing job?'

'No, not plumbing. The hole I'm thinking of is a squared-off bit of empty space.'

'Ah . . . we're on the metaphysical plane, are we?'

'Maybe. Our colour's gone. The box is away.'

'And you with it. Are you destroyed?'

'No, but it makes you think.'

Byers folded his paper impatiently and held it together in one hand while he adjusted his glasses the better to see a clock some blocks farther up the street. He was a reader. In the evenings, after listening for a certain self-specified time to the complaints of customers who rang him about his paper-boys, he would go off to the library – the phone still ringing behind him. Once there he would go through a further set of papers and magazines and return near closing-time with a pile of books under his arm. Garrad sensed the impatience of this man, but he went on:

'It makes you wonder about what's real and what isn't. Or whether it's all one. A TV tree and the one outside the window, for instance. Would it matter if you never saw the outside one again? Or is it better?'

'So we're on to morals now,' said Byers. 'Good, bad and better has nothing to do with it.'

'Maybe not. But I want to be sure I *feel* the difference between them.'

'Pleasure's all that matters. The thing that gives you most – that's the one to go for.' There was a silence. Byers again held his paper up and they were joined by an old woman who scanned the headlines for a moment, decided against the full version, and shuffled off.

'Women have this way of skimming the cream off everything,' said Byers, 'and at the same time they get it for nothing. But you were saying?'

'Real and unreal. The other day, coming out of a restaurant, I bent down to a table and tried to smell a vase of those pink and white carnations. Oh, very real *they* were! As I sniffed several people sitting near saw me, and guffawed.'

'And what of it?'

'It was a very unpleasant sensation. What next? I thought. Maybe next time I'll be asking the way of a scarecrow. I was afraid it would grow on me – mixing up real and unreal. I didn't feel one hundred per cent human.'

'Well, who is? Don't worry. And concentrate on pleasure.'

Garrad stared at him, at his melancholy mouth, down-turned as though by the continual drag of dark headlines which he held beneath his chin.

'So you've no colour,' Byers said suddenly as Garrad was moving quietly away. 'Better try walking westwards.'

In the west it was smouldering up into a sunset, not yet in full blaze. There was already a glow around him, but Garrad's thoughts were grey. He felt some loneliness walking back by himself in the pale pink. Even his own talk of real and unreal had unnerved him a bit. He'd been lucky to meet a few people. But he needed more than that. He was turning in now to a long street of identical houses whose front-room windows were so close to the pavement you could almost touch the glass by stretching over one strip of grass narrow as a doormat. The difference between one place and the next lay mainly in these green doormats – some were well-groomed and plushy, others threadbare or dotted with daisies. Now the pink light, growing deeper, illumined house-fronts, stained smooth doorsteps, and glinted over-head from a thick bristling of aerials. Most curtains were still undrawn and he had a full view into front rooms. He went more slowly. Most had already switched on. In some rooms there were families, in others single persons – all bathed in a mixture of sunset pink and ghostly TV light. At one house the box flickered over an empty room. Garrad stood staring at a fisherman until a woman appeared in the doorway, stood and watched the fisherman for a time, and went out again. Again she came back, switched from fisherman to skyscrapers to a shampooed head and back to the fisherman. She went out again and Garrad moved on. The fisherman was now on most sets and on one in four screens he was in colour. It made a fine colour-picture. The fisherman was knee-deep in a river on a summer evening, and it was an evening which seemed to keep step with the actual evening outside. The river was flowing pink just as the pavement where Garrad walked was beginning to glow. He went more and more slowly. Where groups sat he saw only profiles and backs of heads and at one or two open windows heard snatches of screen commentary. Here whole families were sitting spellbound or bound by boredom. He had the feeling that if he stepped over and tapped on these windows not a head would turn. If a head *did* turn and he beckoned – who would exert the strongest pull? He with his sunset behind him or the fisherman with his? He felt unfairly matched, for he was now tired. He imagined he made a rather poor picture compared with the rapt riverman. Not even switched on. To all intents and purposes, though with the red behind him, an invisible man.

Garrad was three-quarters down this long street when he met his match. A dozen houses or so from the end he turned his head towards one wide window and saw – himself. He was set up like all the rest of them, handsomely framed and mounted – the same for size, the same for clarity. His background glowed out stronger and redder even than the fisherman's. He was looking into a mirror which stood squarely in that place where in all other rooms he had looked for the TV set. It was an old-fashioned mirror set up on a stand, like a picture on a short easel, and placed on a side-table well away from the wall. The room itself was identical to all the other rooms of the street. Yet in atmosphere it was different. It lacked the sealed-off, all-absorbed look of the others. Here there was no spellbinder – only two young women who, their backs to the window, were bending over the end of a long table. It wasn't easy to see what they were doing. They might be wrapping and tying a dumpy parcel from the look of it, or pressing and persuading a yeasty roll of dough. They stood aside for a moment and he saw a baby being zipped into a nightsack. Its head rolled upon the tabletop. Its furious feet made the corners of the bag squirm like a flame-curled envelope. Garrad watched the performance. For more than half the street he'd been an invisible screen-watcher, familiar only with the backs of heads. But now one of the women, catching sight of his head in the mirror, twisted round to face him. This double look fascinated Garrad. At one blow he was twice hailed, twice identified as a living man. Now the other woman had turned. As though aware of some oddness in their background, lacking a TV, they did more than turn their heads. They seemed amused at the man gaping in at them. One of them swung the baby in its bag up off the table and both came to the window and pushed it wider open. Garrad leaned on the gate. The baby was balanced on the window ledge, its white woollen bag absorbing sunset like a sponge.

'Talk about fire!' exclaimed the young mother leaning out. 'That sky is quite something!'

'The best I've seen for years,' Garrad replied.

'He's never seen one yet,' she said, hitching the baby farther up. 'It's his first, I believe. This *is* his first.' Garrad felt that only with reluctance had the baby let his fury subside. At any moment it might burst again. Meanwhile it continued to stare out.

'It's not the sky that interests him,' said the other, who was obviously a sister. 'I don't believe he'd so much as blink if the sky turned suddenly green or black or whatever. *People* interest him.'

'He loves *colour*. And I believe he even looks at distance,' said the mother. Stern and impassive, the baby hung between them while they bickered gently behind his back. There was some jealousy around. Even Garrad felt jealous for himself. He had alerted them to colour. He *was* colour. His shoulders and back were saturated with it, his hair pronged with pink. Between their shoulders he got a glimpse of himself in the mirror with great streaks of fire behind his head.

'Yes, it was seeing you in *that*,' said the sister following his glance. 'If you hadn't stopped just where you are we wouldn't have noticed until too late. It's past its best already, isn't it?' Garrad was appeased. He was about to move on when there was a flash of lightning and some moments later a distant rumble of thunder.

'Oh I knew that was coming!' said the girl holding the baby. There was another flash behind Garrad's left shoulder followed directly by a much louder boom. The women at the window were now staring at him transfixed. He was something now all right with his flaming sky and lightning springing between his shoulders. For a moment all three were satisfied to stare – the women at the sudden drama outside, the man at the scene indoors. But the baby, peeved by the momentary withdrawal of attention, began to girn and twist in its bag.

'You'll excuse us if we shut the window now,' said its mother. 'But thanks – thanks for drawing our attention . . .'

Garrad waved. He saw his own hand move in their mirror and got again the double response, as they faced him and as they turned inwards and saw his image. He moved away, past more family groups, past couples and single viewers. The fisherman had long ago packed up and a dozen soldiers were galloping with spears poised through a narrow gorge between mountains. Thunder was rumbling very far off. Garrad walked slowly though he was still a long way from his own part of the town. The fiery sky was already half extinguished, but for a short time the colour down in the streets seemed deeper than ever as though trapped and richly mixed with dark stone or floating through the dust and soot in the air. By the time Garrad reached his district the whole upper sky had faded to a yellow-green, but here and there between the distant cranes and spires on the town's horizon there were still some streaks of orange light. He turned another corner, walked up a long street of empty offices and shops and out into the part where the double villas and careful gardens began. He was near home. A few steps farther and he was looking into his own front room. The place was lit but deserted and the square of emptiness where the TV had stood seemed more conspicuous than ever. Yet as soon as he was inside he knew the heavy atmosphere had fractionally lifted. A moment later his wife came through from the back of the house.

'The colour's coming back!' she said.

'It's what?'

'They phoned soon after you left. And there's not all that much wrong. We'll have the colour back first thing to-morrow.'

'Well, thank God for that.' His gratitude for the returning colour-box sounded thin to his own ears. The very flatness of his tone gave the lie to it. Yet when it did come tomorrow wouldn't he welcome colour back with open arms? He didn't doubt it. At this moment, however, he was loaded with the stuff himself. The new substance. The real thing. His clothes were soaked in it to the skin. The whole gamut of reds had penetrated to his bone-marrow and was now thickening his blood. But he was not, as far as he could see, radiating any of this spectacular substance himself. His wife looked blank. The hall was dim and getting dimmer. On his right hung a large mirror and on the opposite side a smaller one reflecting to infinity a square of biscuit-toned wall. Between these Garrad moved forward carefully but stopped at the foot of the stairs. His wife was watching him closely.

'What are you thinking about?' she said.

'Colour, of course.'

'Are you thinking about the missing colour?'

'No, just colour.'

'*Not* the missing colour?'

'No. Colour.'

'What, to be exact?'

'The usual. Starting with that odd tree that sticks out into the road. Never noticed before but it's got half its bark peeled off. Every boy who passes tears a strip. It's white on the pavement side, black on the other. It's a cartoon tree now.'

'Black and white? Are you still talking about colour?'

'I went past the market. Rails and rails of red, blue and yellow dresses. Who buys them?'

'What's so *new*?'

'Nothing. I went as far as the school with the glass. There's actually a palm-tree in the corridor. Imagine it! There'll not be much stripped off *that* one. And back again. The stalls were packing up. People fingering huge piles of bashed plums and split tomatoes.' He paused.

'What else?'

Garrad had his foot on the stairs. 'The sky.' He drew his breath with a slight hiss. 'There's still a patch.'

'A patch?'

'Of red. Of pink now. You might still see something from the back room. One patch left, and getting smaller every minute.' He started to go up. His wife who had been staring at him as though expecting the knobs of his backbone to light up, now stood reluctantly pondering the pale pink patch, her foot on the bottom stair. Slowly she went up after him.

6

ALAN SPENCE

GYPSY

'Gypsies ur worse than cathlicks!' said Shuggie to Aleck. 'Nae kiddin. They huvnae a fuckin clue.'

Les the gypsy said nothing. He just laughed and carried on tearing open packets of jotters and stacking them on an old table. The storeroom was thick with dust and a yellow winter light filtered in through the one window, which was small and grimy with bars on the outside. There was a single lightbulb but it had fused and the janitor hadn't got round to replacing it.

Shuggie and Aleck were savouring the few minutes of freedom from the classroom, clambering over packing-cases and ancient desks, all chipped and battered, scrawled on and carved. They climbed and rummaged, poked and dug, from the highest shelf to the darkest grubbiest corner, expecting always to unearth some fabled, long-lost treasure.

But Les insisted on going on with the work they'd been sent to do. That was what rankled Shuggie, though he hated the gypsy anyway.

'Wotcha think yer gonna find?' asked Les.

'Wojja finkya gonna foind?' said Shuggie, mocking his English accent.

'Very funny,' said Les.

'Vewy fanny,' said Shuggie. 'Anywey, never you mind whit. Jist you wait an see.'

69

'Some'dy funn a stuffed owl wance,' said Aleck. 'In a glass case it wis. An some'dy else funn a dead dead dead auld fotie a the Rangers.'

'Whit ye talkin tae that cunt fur?' said Shuggie.

'Ach c'mon,' said Aleck. 'E's no daein any herm. Ah mean wu've goat tae soart oot the jotters sometime.'

'Aw ah'm sayin is thur's nae hurry,' said Shuggie. 'We kin take wur time. Nae need tae belt intae it as if wur daein piecework.'

'Ach well,' said Aleck. There was a silence. Then he went on, telling Les. 'An thur's supposed tae be gas-masks, an fitba strips, an bladders, an loads a great books, an jist . . . hunners a things!'

'Must be pretty well hidden!' said Les, looking round the room and laughing.

'Smartarse!' said Shuggie, then, turning to Aleck, 'D'ye wanty gie tit-features a haun then?'

'Aw right,' said Aleck, jumping down from the desk-top where he was squatting. He lifted down a packet of jotters and tore it open.

The jotters were all a dingy brown colour with the Highway Code on the front. On the back were the multiplication tables and lists of weights and measures, to be memorised. Aleck was reading over the rules for road safety. He had never really thought about them before, though he must have looked at the words a million times. DANGER! DANGER! DANGER! At the kerb HALT! That was like the Lifeboys. By the left, Quick MARCH! Aleck hated the stupid marching and drill. He really went to the Lifeboys for the football. NEVER play games on the street. Where else was there to play? Mrs Stone their teacher was always on about keeping them off the streets. She was new at the school and she wanted to organise sports for them. She said it was good for them to be in the Lifeboys or the Cubs.

Healthy. Shuggie had been in the Cubs once but he'd been put out for stealing a scout-knife and fighting over it in the hall. Now whenever he saw Aleck with his Lifeboy uniform he had a good laugh at it. Called him sailor-boy.

'Aleck!' Shuggie's voice was muffled as if he was shouting from down a hole. He had crawled along under the desks to get at a low cupboard in a far corner of the room. He was kneeling there, hunched, coughing and choking on the dust he'd stirred up.

'Gonnae see if ye kin find a stick ur somethin,' he said.

Aleck looked around the room. 'Wid a ruler dae?' he asked.

'It wid prob'ly brek,' said Shuggie. 'Somethin a wee bit heavier.'

Aleck looked again and this time found a broken pointer. He held up the two bits. 'Prob'ly cracked ower somedy's skull!' he said.

'Likely enough,' said Les.

'See if this'll dae,' said Aleck, passing the pointed end in to Shuggie.

'Great!' said Shuggie. He wedged it in at the jamb of the door and tried to prise it open. There was a loud crack as something splintered and broke. He ducked his head from another shower of dust, and the door flapped back on its hinges.

When the dust had settled he began scrabbling and groping in the cupboard. Then he let out a yell. 'Aleck! C'mere an . . . Jesus! Wait tae ye see this!'

Aleck hurried over, stooping down to peer under the desks as Shuggie came struggling out, backwards, feet first. He was dragging with him a cardboard box. Aleck tried to see what was in it. He could make out some colour, red and white, a streak of yellow. Then Shuggie was out and up on his feet, lifting the box clear, into the light.

'Therr!' he said, laying it down on the floor.

Aleck looked and couldn't believe it. The box was full of football jerseys, the old style, with collars. They had red and white stripes. On top was a goalkeeper's jersey, yellow. Aleck knelt down, open-mouthed, bright-eyed. He touched one of the jerseys, softly. It didn't disappear. It was real. He let out a long slow breath, full of amazement and wonder.

'D'ye think ther's a full set?' he said at last, grinning up at Shuggie.

'Mibbe,' said Shuggie, grinning back. 'Mon wull count them.' He began, lifting them out and passing them to Aleck. They handled each one gently, lovingly, fearful in case such a treasure should crumble away.

'Ten,' said Aleck, 'an a goalie's jersey!'

'A whole fuckin team!' said Shuggie.

'They've git numbers an everythin!' said Aleck, laying them down beside the jotters.

Shuggie searched through the pile till he found the number nine jersey. He draped it over his shoulders, the sleeves hanging down at the front, then he side-stepped past Les and dribbled the cardboard box across the floor.

'Jist a minnit,' said Aleck. 'Whit ur we gonnae dae wi thum?'

'Ah wis thinkin,' said Shuggie. 'Listen. Ye know how auld Stoney's always oan aboot sports an that. Ah think we could get ur tae let us huv a team.'

'God!' said Aleck. 'D'ye think she wid?'

'Sure,' said Shuggie. 'Wu'll take thum back up wi us an you kin ask ur.'

'How me?' said Aleck.

'Och c'mon!' said Shuggie. 'She likes you. You're good at compositions an that.'

'Aw right,' said Aleck. 'Ah'll ask ur. C'mon, we better get back up before ther's a search-party oot lookin fur us.'

Shuggie placed the jerseys carefully back in the box.

'Tellt ye we'd find somethin din't ah!' he said to Les.

'We better not forget the jotters,' said Les.

'Ach!' said Shuggie. 'Whit did ah tell ye, Aleck? Gypsies ur ignorant. Pure fuckin ignorant.'

'So you just happened to find them on a shelf while you were looking for the jotters?' said Mrs Stone.

'Yes miss!' said Shuggie and Aleck, together. She didn't look convinced.

'How did you get yourself so dirty, Hugh?' she asked Shuggie. He had dusted himself down, but he still looked far from clean. Somehow he had managed to smear a lopsided moustache across his upper lip.

'Ther wis a lot a dust 'n tap a the boax, miss.' he said.

'On TOP of the BOX,' she said. 'Not on tap of the boax! Some of these days I'll manage to teach you children some English!'

But she was glad that the jerseys had been found. And it was agreed, they were to have a team. She would arrange a few friendly games for them with other schools and youth clubs. But first they were to have a trial match. They were to pick two teams, a first and a second. The trial was fixed for the coming Saturday. But for now they had to give out the jotters. They had grammar to learn.

The rest of the afternoon dragged. Aleck kept looking out the high window at the grey sky, dreaming, not really hearing Mrs Stone's droning voice, wishing they were free so he could talk to the others about the team. He glanced across the passage at Shuggie. Inside the cover of his new jotter, he was drawing a football player, in a striped jersey, with a number nine on the back.

They were not real gypsies, only people who travelled with

the shows, moving from fairground to fairground, all over Scotland and England, and sometimes across to Ireland. But theirs was a wandering life and they lived in caravans, so people called them gypsies or tinkers.

When they came to Glasgow, they lived on a rise of waste ground, backing on to a railway line, across the road from the school. Here they stayed for two or three months every winter, when the shows were at Kelvin Hall or Glasgow Green.

The rise of ground had come to be called Gypsy's Hill. Along the crest of it was a high wooden fence, each section about a foot wide and thick enough to stand on, dark wood, rotted and weathered by the years. The fence ran right round the gypsies' encampment like a great stockade, enclosing it.

At the foot of this stockade, Aleck and Shuggie were playing. The ground had frozen over and they had been trying to smooth a part of the slope, taking turns at sliding down it on a makeshift sledge, a chunk of linoleum they'd dragged out of a midden. But now the sun was growing warmer, thawing out the ground. Only the part of the hill in the shadow of the fence remained frozen, hard. There was practically a straight line, the line of the shadow, dividing this part from the rest, already growing soft and muddy.

Aleck noticed it, the strangeness of it, and pointed it out to Shuggie.

'Weird that, intit,' he said.

'So it is,' said Shuggie.

Neither of them had ever seen the like. The line was so definite, the division so sharp.

'Bet ye that's thae gypsies,' said Shuggie.

'How d'ye mean?' said Aleck.

'Hauf ae thum's witches an that,' said Shuggie. 'They know aw aboot magic an spells an stuff.'

'Fortune tellin,' said Aleck.

'Tell'n ye,' said Shuggie, 'therr's prob'ly aw kinds a bad magic aboot here. That's how the grun's still aw frozen here an naewherr else.'

They looked up at the fence, looming, the thick upright sections like standing stones against the bright, watery sky.

'Ma da says gypsies wid cut yer throat for a penny,' said Shuggie. 'Thur always kidnappin weans tae.'

Aleck didn't really believe it. He shivered, but only from the cold. He remembered from somewhere a bit of a poem.

My mother said I never should
Play with gypsies in the wood.

Never play games on the street. Never follow a ball, hoop or playmate.

'Think wur gonnae go up in a puff a smoke any minute?' he said, laughing.

'Naaa!' said Shuggie. 'Ah'm no feart fae gypsies ur tinkers ur naebody!' and he went to the foot of the fence, Aleck following. They went to where there was a knot-hole a couple of feet from the ground. The hole had been worn away and was big enough for a foot-hold. Aleck crouched down and peered through.

'There's wee Valerie,' he said. Shuggie crouched down beside him.

Valerie was another reason Shuggie hated the gypsies, especially Les. She too was in their class at school. She had blonde hair, long and soft, parted in the middle and tied back from her face. Shuggie had always fancied her, but she had no time for him. She preferred Les, another gypsy, English like herself. They watched her now, framed by the rough oval of the hole in the fence. She was playing at shops, by herself. She had a few old bottles, filled with dirt and small stones. She was emptying these onto scraps of newspaper, wrapping them into small parcels and arranging them along the wooden steps leading to the door of a caravan. They watched her, moving before them, lost in her own world. Then Shuggie put his fingers to his lips and let out a piercing whistle. She looked up but couldn't see them. She was too far away and the hole was too small. She went back to her game.

Shuggie climbed up onto the fence and reaching down helped Aleck up after him. They sat, straddling the fence, their legs dangling down on either side. From here they could see the whole camp spread out, huge vans and lorries, caravans with windows and doors and smoke rising from tin chimneys, gruff-looking men and women, going about their mysterious business, everywhere children and dogs.

Shuggie called out Valerie's name in a high-pitched, mocking voice. She looked up, saw them and turned her back, very deliberately going on playing. He called out again. This time she went up the steps into the caravan and a moment later a man came out. He had a thick sandy moustache. He was dressed in dungarees. He waved his fist and shouted at them. 'Gaan! Get dahn ourra that!'

Shuggie gave him the V-sign, a last act of bravado, but as he started towards them they were glad to scramble down from the fence, down to the foot of the hill and clear across the back-courts, scared that the man would strike them down with a curse, shrivel them to ashes as they ran.

Saturday morning was clear and cold. Shuggie and Aleck were the first to arrive at the pitches, at the far end of Bellahouston Park. Four or five other games were already under way and the sounds carried over, the sounds that were always so strangely empty in such an open space. Voices shouting. Leather against leather. Shuggie had brought his ball, specially dubbined and laced, blown up hard. They tapped it about to each other while they waited and gradually the others arrived, singly and in small groups. Mrs Stone was there to act as referee, and a few girls from the school, to watch. The teams had been picked from their class, which was the qualifying, and the one below. The first team had already been issued with the jerseys and they all wore their strips under their other clothes which they just had to slip off to be ready. Some had boots, others made do with heavy shoes.

Among the girls was Valerie, who had come with Les. Les was at left back for the second team. Shuggie was at centre forward for the first team, Aleck at outside right. The jerseys were all the one size so Aleck's was too big for him, the sleeves coming down over his hands, and Shuggie's was a bit tight, the cuffs stopping short of his big bony wrists. They laughed at each other. Aleck pranced up and down like a male model and Shuggie threw the ball after him, both performing for the girls watching as well as for each other.

At last they were ready and the game began.

They played half an hour each way, stopping for five minutes at half time. The frozen bone-hard pitch was rutted and uneven, the grass rough and sparse, and the ball difficult to control, especially for the bigger, heavier defence of the second team, who floundered and grew more shaky and haphazard as the game went on. The other team were generally more nimble, surer on their feet, and in the end they won easily by six goals to two, Shuggie scoring three. At the final whistle they leapt in the air, threw up their arms, rushed to hug and slap each other on the back. It didn't matter that it was just a stupid trial. They had won. They were entitled to strut and parade in their glorious red and white.

Mrs Stone had to go then. That was why the game hadn't been a full ninety minutes. But most of the boys decided to stay and play on.

'Wonderful game, boys!' said Mrs Stone. 'Wonderful! I'll be seeing you all on Monday morning then. And don't forget to bring back the jerseys.'

They re-shuffled the teams, to make things a bit more even. Four of the boys had gone so they were down to nine-a-side.

They had been playing about twenty minutes when the ball broke to Aleck just on the halfway line. He pushed it through the middle and Shuggie ran onto the pass, but Les had moved back to cover. As he came in to tackle, Shuggie dummied to the left. This should have left Les stranded and off balance, but he was slow and instead of following Shuggie's feint, he lunged forward clumsily, missing the ball, catching Shuggie below the knee with a heavy tackety boot. Carried forward by their own momentum they collided, crashing together and falling to the ground.

Shuggie was up first, hobbling, gritting his teeth against the pain in his leg, easing it by spitting out a steady rhythmic barrage at Les.

'Gan ya durty fuckin black enamel bastard ye!'

Les was just getting to his feet when Shuggie threw the first punch, catching him on the jaw and laying him out again. Then Les was up and they were swinging at each other. A few of the other boys tried to break it up and pull them apart. The girls were shrieking with delighted horror. The ball had rolled a few yards away and lay where it came to rest, unnoticed and forgotten.

On Monday morning some of the girls had been talking to Mrs Stone. She was looking grim and righteous as she sent Aleck next door to fetch the boys from the other class who had played in the trial. 'And tell those who have jerseys to bring them,' she said. The others had been called out to the floor in front of her desk, without explanation. They waited, shuffling, awkward. She went on with some corrections. When Aleck came back with the rest she put down her pen and looked at them.

Then she began. The girls had told her about the scuffle, about the amount of swearing that had gone on.

'And I was disgusted,' she said. 'It seems I just can't turn my back on you for a minute but you're behaving like the lowest of animals. You've really disappointed me, boys. If that's a sample of your behaviour then you just can't be trusted. And I'm certainly not willing to make any effort for a bunch of hooligans who are just going to disgrace me. So that's it, boys. No more football, and you've only yourselves to blame.'

She brought out the cardboard box and laid it down in front of her desk.

'Those of you who have jerseys,' she went on, 'put them back in the box. The boys from next door, go back to your class. The rest of you sit down and get out your arithmetic jotters. Hugh and Leslie, stay where you are. I hear you were the worst offenders.' She reached into the desk for her belt.

'Actually brawling!' she said. 'Just think yourselves lucky I don't send you to the headmaster. Right Leslie, you first. Cross your hands.'

She belted them both twice. She sent Les back to his seat and told Shuggie to pick up the box of jerseys.

'You will take these jerseys,' she said, 'and put them back where you found them, and I will hear no more about football from any of you.'

They were numbed. She had pronounced sentence, and they knew that it was final.

'Right!' she said, turning to the class. 'Arithmetic.'

Gypsy's Touch was a sadistic kind of tig-game that had been

dreamed up by Shuggie. Somebody would brush against Les or another gypsy, and jump back as if contaminated. The aim of the game then was to transfer the infection, by touch, to somebody else who would try to pass it on again.

Now that they all blamed Les for the collapse of their dreams of having a football team, the game was more popular.

Shuggie jostled Les in the dinner-hall queue and recoiled.

'Gypsy's Touch!' he gasped out, clutching his hand to his throat, then poking somebody else and beginning the game. The queue broke up in disorder as they chased and ran, ducked and climbed, desperate to avoid the Touch.

'D'ye know whit happens when ye get Gypsy's Touch?' shouted Shuggie.

They delighted in trying to imagine.

'Ye turn intae a gypsy an they come an take ye away!'

'Ye go aff yer heid an kill yer maw an da!'

'Ye get covered in plooks!'

'Yer skin turns green!'

'Ye get scabies!'

'Warts!'

'Worms!'

'Nits!'

'Boils!'

'Dysentry!'

'Leprosy!'

'Black Death!'

'THE DREADED LERGY!'

And at this last, the ultimate affliction, they all joined in a strangled cry and gave up trying to better each other, because no more could be added. There could be nothing worse than the Lergy. It included all the rest, and more.

And all Les could do was turn away from them, and try to let none of it touch him, for the playground was their territory, and no place for him to get into another fight.

On Friday night Shuggie and Aleck set out early for the shows. They took the subway, two stops, to Partick Cross and walked up to the Kelvin Hall.

They paid their money, pushed open the big heavy glass-panelled doors and passed through into another world. It didn't matter that the money they had was meagre and wouldn't last. They were here, and the whole carnival was spread out glittering before them. It was all theirs, and they swaggered, feeling the weight of the coins that jingled in their pockets, and their only problem was where to begin.

'C'mon, wull find the Ghost Train!' said Shuggie.

The tiny green-painted train crashed through the tin doors and trundled into the darkness and the tape-recorded shrieks and siren-wails and howls. And it gathered speed and hurtled towards a succession of mechanical, wobbling figures, brightly lit for a moment as the train ran straight towards them, and always just in time lurched clear round another bend in the track, and the lights went out and the darkness swallowed the figures again, spectres and spooks, skeletons and ghouls, corpses, vampires, bodysnatchers with skulls, giant spiders, bats and owls, all vanished till they were switched on again for the next train coming through. And the screams and low moans faded as the doors bashed open before them and they were back out into the brightness and noise of the main hall and the ride was over.

'Wisnae very frightenin, wis it?' said Shuggie.

And they moved on. They climbed the helter skelter, they spun on the rotor, flattened against the wall as the floor dropped away beneath their feet; they guzzled ice-lollies and lemonade, potato crisps and candy floss; they rocked almost head over heels on the ribtickler.

'Ah feel a wee bit sick,' said Aleck.

'D'ye wanty sit doon?' said Shuggie.

'Ach naw,' said Aleck. 'Ah'll be aw right in a minnit.'

'C'mon, wull look at the mirrors,' said Shuggie. 'Ye better no take any merr shooglin aboot jist the noo.'

In the Hall of Mirrors they joined the hysterical laughing procession, convulsed and doubled up, howling with disbelief and glee at their own warped reflections. Here they were squashed to a blubbery dumpiness; here they were stretched and elongated; here their heads split in two; here eyes, noses, teeth all merged; they moved and their images rippled, changed shape, broke up and came together again, wobbled across the surface of the glass like globules of oil, like jelly, like treacle dripped from a spoon. They were still laughing as they came to the last mirror and saw there two small shabby-looking boys laughing back at them. Aleck recognised one of them as Shuggie and eventually the other as himself. It felt strange for a moment. But they pointed at the glass and laughed again, as if this too was a distortion.

Out again, they ran to the rockets. The sign said Space Trip above painted moons and planets.

They lifted off into orbit and spun towards the roofbeams and the rafters, the empty gloom above the hall, and Aleck wished his ship could break free from the machine and he could sail out through a secret escape-hatch (known only to him) and zoom across the river to Govan, dip and loop over his friends' astonished upturned faces, mad with envy as he dropped a bomb on the school. He would soar past their third-story tenement window, waving as his mother dropped the teapot and his father gaped out from behind his newspaper, and they would call him back for his supper, but he would just laugh and go on, higher and higher, and never stop. But as they slowed and came to rest, again he was feeling sick. Shuggie counted out the money he had left.

'Uv you goat the same as me?' he asked.

'Jist aboot,' said Aleck.

'That means wu've goat wur subway ferrs an enough fur anuther coupla hurls,' said Shuggie.

Aleck was looking across at a group of stalls and at one of them he saw Valerie, taking in the money. The game she had charge of was to lob rubber balls into upturned enamel buckets. Aleck pointed her out to Shuggie.

'Fancy tryin wur luck?' said Shuggie.

'Might win somethin ah suppose,' said Aleck. They sauntered over.

'Haya Valerie!' said Shuggie, hoping others would notice his casual familiarity.

'Three balls a tanner,' she said, coldly.

Aleck paid and Shuggie watched him waste all three balls. The first went in and bounced straight out again. The second hit the rim. The third missed the bucket altogether.

'Ach!' said Shuggie, shoving him. 'Useless! C'mon, ah'll show ye how it's done.' They moved on to the next stall. Wild West Aunt Sally it was called. Three balls to throw at a row of wooden faces, alternate Indians and Outlaws, scowling and mean. They both recognised the stallholder as the man that had chased them down from the fence at Gypsy's Hill, but he gave no sign that he remembered them.

Shuggie's first throw knocked over an outlaw. His second sent an Indian spinning. 'Nae bother!' he said. He spat on his hands. He had already selected his prize, a red vinyl football, nestling among the racks of teddybears and tea-sets, gilt mirrors and jigsaws, stacks of knick-knacks and toys.

He drew back his arm like a baseball pitcher and threw. The ball smacked against the Indian's flat wooden face; the face wobbled but didn't tilt and just stared back at them, meaner than ever.

'Ard luck mate,' said the man, handing him a consolation prize, a white plaster poodle.

'Wait a minnit!' said Shuggie. 'Ah hut that fuckin thing an it never went ower!'

'C'mon now sonny,' said the man. 'That's the luck o the game, innit?'

'Bet yis widnae try that wi a man,' said Shuggie. 'Shower a pochlin bastards!'

Valerie had called the man over and whispered something in his ear. He looked angrier as he turned to them.

'So it's you two again, eh! Bloody little troublemakers. Go on. Gerraway! Hoppit before I ave yer put out!'

There was nothing they could do so they moved off, Shuggie still angry, scowling back and muttering.

They saw Valerie crossing to a lucky-dip stall called Aladdin's Cave and there behind the counter was Les. She spoke to him and pointed over, laughing, to where they stood, and Les laughed too.

'Gonnae get that cunt on Monday,' said Shuggie, quietly.

'Ye kin gie yer maw the dug,' said Aleck.

'Look at it,' said Shuggie, disgusted. 'A fuckin poodle.'

The back of the ornament was flat, unfinished, chalky.

'Kin use it fur writin on the wa',' said Shuggie, resigning himself to it. They were standing next to the Waltzers. 'Comin oan these?' he said.

'Awright,' said Aleck. 'Then that'll be us skint an we kin go hame.'

As they climbed in, Aleck suddenly felt sad that their money was gone and they hadn't seen the circus animals; the elephants, monkeys, horses and all the rest that made up the Carnival Zoo. But he soon forgot as the Waltzers started up and the dizziness came back, the tightness in his head and the nausea rising slow. They went faster and faster, spinning and hurling and he had to cling tight, gripping the metal bar. The screams and laughter and the grinding music were suddenly more than he could bear. The journey was never going to end. He would whirl and buck forever in this brash tinny hell. He wanted nothing more than to get off.

The ride at last came to a stop and he tottered from the machine. But it made no difference. It was just another nightmare. He wanted to be home and safe in his bed without the journey back through grey dismal streets. But he was here. The fair that had seemed so beautiful and full of wonders was the foulest place on earth. The ground was unsteady beneath his trembling legs. He sweated and shook. He wanted to be home but he was here and it was real. The clanking music jarred, discordant, pounding in his head. Stupid names, Space Trip, Aladdin's Cave. Faces, laughing, hostile, every one ugly and harsh. Fairy lights stuttering round and round his brain, a persistent annoying rhythm.

As he slumped down against a litter-bin, Shuggie realised he was sick. 'Godalmighty,' he said. 'Ye look green.' Aleck groaned.

'Shows is a terrible place fur that,' went on Shuggie. 'Ah wance saw a fulla bein sick aff the chairaplane. Jist a big stream a honk flyin oot. Folk hid tae jump oot the road so they widnae get splattered!'

Aleck turned away, retched and heaved, and up it came. The final racking misery before he could be purged and clear.

He stood up shakily, wiping away the tears from his face, and his eyes focused on Valerie and Les and the man with the sandy moustache. They were talking together and laughing and he knew they were laughing at him, and he knew they must have poisoned him with their black gypsy magic.

Shuggie saw where he was looking and clapped his arm round his shoulder.

'C'mon hame Aleck,' he said. 'Yu'll feel better oot'n the fresh err.'

Outside the pubs were just emptying. They hadn't realised it was so late. They walked down to Partick Cross in silence and subdued.

7

THE LESSON

ONCE MORE the boy is standing on the hassock. The hassock is plump and blue. It is covered in a special sort of velvet that looks as if it has maps in it. The hassock stands in the bay window of the long room. You can tell from the sun on the books that it is evening. There is no need for a fire but there is a fire. The fire's flicker is making the round oak table glow and the flames are reflected in the violin also. The boy is holding the violin half tenderly, half fearfully. He is frightened of the music. He is a fat bashful boy, his hair is combed straight over his forehead. The tutor is standing with his back to the room, looking out, his hands clasped behind his back. His clever grey eyes are veined with blood. The lower part of the tutor's face is soft and voluptuous, while the upper part might have been dug out of a bit of wood with a penknife. The tutor is watching the buzzard. The buzzard's squared tail is barred black and brown. It is turning slowly, very high, the sun on its wings.

The tutor's mouth is opening. A thin elastic of saliva connects his lips. Now the saliva breaks and words fall out. The glass mists. Through the windowpane the long lawn mists, and the cypress trees. 'We'll try again.'

The boy has a pebble in his pocket. He can feel it pressing against his leg through the thin stuff of his trousers. Some of the books in the bookcase have their names blocked in gold.

The tutor sucks at the hollow tooth on the left side of his mouth. It tastes faintly of oranges. 'Think.'

The boy says nothing. He sighs, just perceptibly, the shoulders of his tight jacket rising and falling no more than half an inch. His hair is cropped close against his skull at the sides, then combed straight forward. His shoes against the hassock are the colour of red squirrels. He has a pasty face. He sighs again. He sighs a lot. He is always sighing, the boy, nothing animates him. He is moving his hands now on the violin. They are white and inadequate on the rich wood.

'The bow,' the tutor is saying, 'the bow *must* be drawn steadily to its point, it has to be parallel with the bridge, precisely parallel, so that the wrist is compelled –'

Beyond the bay window, through the breath-stained glass, at the end of the long lawn, just level with the statue of Pomona with the breasts like little apples, there is a hare that has come into the garden. The tutor did not see her enter, but now that she is there he has noticed her. The hare's ears have black tips. They shiver as rain starts, quite heavily, then stops again. With every twig that creaks in the hedge the hare's bones jump under her scraggy skin, her muscles pump her far away although she is not moving. The tutor's grey eyes note her trembling. 'Compelled,' he is saying. 'And at the end of the stroke,' he is saying, 'on reaching the point of the bow, the wrist should *sink*, so that the little finger only rests at its extreme tip upon the stick.'

The boy has slightly protruding eyes. His eyes are glassy with concentration now as he tries to make his disobedient fingers do what they are told. But it is no good. The bow squeals on the string. The boy is blushing. The tutor's eyes are bloodshot. He is taking a quick suck of whisky from a small pearl-stoppered flask, then he is slipping the flask back again in an inside pocket of his black frockcoat. A cravat mounts to his chin, pinned by a narrow silver pin twisted in

a double bar. There is something almost coquettish about
the way the hare is holding her head slightly to one side.
There is something flirty and evasive in her sidling glances
across the lawn in the direction of the house.

'Primary bowings,' the tutor is saying. He watches his
breath on the glass, the swelling and shrinking web.
'Primary bowings consist of the grand detaché – '

The hare's eyes are running while her body stands still.
'A rapid detached stroke,' the tutor is saying, not looking
round, 'using the whole bow, quickly executed, so that a
crotchet sounds like a semi-quaver. Next, the singing
stroke – '

There is a smudge of fur tumbling among the dandelions
at the feet of the statue of Pomona with the breasts like little
apples. It catches the tutor's bloodshot eye. The tutor sees
that the smudge is a leveret, playing not far from its mother.
The tutor takes a handkerchief from his breast pocket and
wipes his forehead. The handkerchief smells of aniseed.
'The singing stroke,' the tutor is saying, 'in which the first
contact must be *delicate*, and the single tones follow each
other without interruption. The mertallato or detached
hammered – '

The boy's fingers are stretched and awkward on the
instrument. The boy is feeling his bones against the wood,
against the taut gut. The bowings hurt his hands. His hands
are soft and fat. He keeps nodding absent-mindedly. He is
always nodding, nothing riles him. His tongue moistens his
pink lips. 'Made at the point of the bow,' the tutor is saying,
'without its leaving the string, you understand, so that with
each note the stick is *pressed* or pushed by the thumb in the
direction of the index finger. The detached stroke with the
forearm – ' A barbed black shadow is falling across the hare.
'Which is self-explanatory,' the tutor is saying. The hare is
rearing up. She finds a hole in the air and leaps through it.

'The skipping stroke,' the tutor is saying, with no change of tone, 'made at the middle of the bow – ' But the barbed shadow is not for the hare. 'The bow,' the tutor is saying, 'being *lightly* held between the fingers and controlled by the wrist, and the stick caused – ' It is the buzzard. 'To vibrate strongly,' the tutor is saying. It is the buzzard. 'Finally,' the tutor is saying, 'finally the rebounding or sautillé or *springing* stroke, which differs – ' The buzzard is crashing softly on to the bewildered leveret. 'Differs from the others,' the tutor is saying. The buzzard's claws are snatching at the leveret's neck. 'In that,' the tutor is saying, 'the bow rebounds – ' Wings wrapping over the struggling shivering morsel. 'From the string – ' With a gesture almost of love. '*After* each note.'

Almost of love. The buzzard is loving that leveret as usual. The buzzard is flying low, bearding the sun, holding his victim under him like a loose parcel of bloody washing. 'And is then permitted,' the tutor is saying.

Not once has the buzzard touched the ground. He has ridden the leveret for a second, but that is all. The boy is trying to cry against the taut gut, to make tears splash on the rich red wood of the violin. But he can only clench and unclench his fingers. 'To fall on it again from above,' the tutor is saying.

The tutor is turning from the window. His clever blood-shot eyes are smiling, but his lips are not.

Once more the boy is standing on the hassock. The fire's flicker is making the round oak table glow and the flames are reflected in the violin also. The violin plays all at once a perfect note. The boy's eyes burn, then fill with tears. He looks up. The room looks different to him. It is the same: the books, the fire, the tutor in the window. But through his tears the boy is seeing it newly, everything changed, made clean, baptised.

8

FRED URQUHART

PILGRIMAGES TO THE OLD MANSE

I MADE my second pilgrimage to the Old Manse nineteen years after I made the first. The first time, Teenie Peebles, the maid who had been with Agnes Inglis for so long, was acting as custodian of the house, which had been turned into a museum since the author's death. I don't know why I expected the old woman, who was getting on for seventy then, still to be there on my second visit; but I did, and I said as much to the woman who opened the door.

'Miss Peebles is dead and gone,' she said. 'I have been in charge these ten years.'

She was every inch a châtelaine, a stout, full-bosomed woman in her late forties, with black eyes and a blue rinse. Her shrewd gaze swept past my grubby cyclamen slacks, my old government surplus anorak and my headscarf, even though it had been bought at great cost at Maggy Rouff's in Paris, and settled on my husband. She scrutinised his expensive tweed suit, his short silvery hair, his distinguished appearance, his air of authority. She was satisfied. Every bit of his six feet three inches and sixteen stones proclaimed that he was a gentleman.

'I am Miss Selkirk,' she said. 'Would you be writing a book about Agnes Inglis, sir?'

I laughed. Teenie Peebles had asked almost the same question. My poor husband, who practically never opens a

book, except a third-rate adventure story, and who thinks
Raymond Chandler is highbrow!

'Mary Selkirk?' I asked.

Her eyes became wary. 'Yes, my name is Mary,' she
admitted.

Before I could stop myself I cried: 'You were another
abandoned child.'

I was about twelve or thirteen when I discovered the novels
of Agnes Inglis. I started to read voraciously when I was
seven. We were an Edinburgh working class family, so
there was only a handful of books in the house. I was an
only child. When I went with my parents to visit their
friends, whose houses had as few books as our own, I
borrowed whenever I could. Mrs Oliphant and Annie S.
Swan, a name revered in almost every Scottish home of that
time, were the only Scottish women authors I'd read until I
read Agnes Inglis. I found her purely by chance in the public
library when I was looking for O. Henry. Our English
teacher had recommended him as 'a master of the short
story' and, in my anxiety for culture, I was going to give
him a going-over. None of his books was 'in' but instead,
in the wrong place, there was *A Laird in Old Siena* by Agnes
Inglis. Some critics say this novel is banal. Perhaps the plot
is, but there is nothing banal about the elegant writing: the
complexities of her Jamesian or Proustian style. I picked the
book off the shelf out of curiosity. A quarter of an hour later
I was still reading. I took it home and finished it that
night.

Agnes Inglis's world of urbane, cultured Scots aristocrats
who moved leisurely from Italy to Spain, from Provence to
Baden-Baden was so different from my own that it charmed
me completely. It was a gracious, gentle world where money
was never mentioned, where evidently it was unknown. But

it had something more than that, a nobility, a sensitivity, a truth, a fundamental rock-bottomedness. She wrote about *real* people. I soaked myself in Agnes Inglis, and by the time I went to Edinburgh University I had read and re-read everything she had written and had found out everything I could about her.

I went to the university much against the grain. It was my father who insisted upon my going. He had 'bettered' himself, as they say, by becoming a small tradesman, and he wanted to better his daughter. I really didn't learn anything there that I wouldn't have found out for myself, but I did get a degree, which was useful later on. The only important thing about the university was meeting Elinor Dalziel. We became friends because of our mutual admiration for the work of Agnes Inglis. I don't suppose I'd have met Elinor otherwise, for she belonged to the landed gentry. Apart from her friendship over the past thirty-five years, it was through her that I met her cousin Robert who became my husband: Robert, who hunts and shoots and fishes, yet who withal (a lovely word that Agnes Inglis loved to use) is as gentle as the legendary dove, General and ex-Governor of a colony though he is.

I met him at Elinor's home in Perthshire soon after my nineteenth birthday. My father was so proud when I told him I was to stay for a week in a castle. It was only a small castle, hardly worthy of the name, but its turrets and wings and balconies grew in number every time he spoke about it to his friends. As for me, it was my first experience of gracious living, and I seized it avidly.

When she was young, Elinor's mother had known Agnes Inglis. She had been brought up on an estate in Dumfries-shire near one belonging to the Inglises. Agnes was an only child. She was twenty years older than Mrs Dalziel, so they'd had few contacts; Mrs Dalziel mostly remembered her as a pretty young woman who had kept a small child well supplied with cakes and biscuits whenever their parents met at tea parties. Agnes's parents had died when she was about thirty. She had turned the family house into a home for foundling girls and gone to live in an old manse. She was still living there, and was now – in that year 1937 – a spinster of seventy-seven. 'She's never married, poor thing,' Mrs Dalziel said. 'She seems to have been content with her romantic friendship with Mr Henry James.'

I said: 'I've read some of their letters.'

'A sad exchange,' Mrs Dalziel said. 'You should write to her yourselves. I believe all writers like to get fan mail or whatever it's called.'

Elinor and I composed a letter, asking if we might visit Miss Inglis to express our admiration by word of mouth. Nearly a month later we got a short typewritten note saying she lived the life of a recluse and saw nobody. The signature looked illiterate.

In 1939 Agnes Inglis published her last novel. I meant to write and tell her how much I'd enjoyed it, but war came and Elinor and Robert and I were swept into it. When Agnes Inglis died in 1942 I did not hear it on the wireless, if it were announced, and I never read about it in a newspaper. The war was almost over before I heard.

In 1943 I married Robert. When the war ended he was posted to Germany; we lived there until 1949. Then we went to Saudi Arabia where he was military adviser to King Ibn Saud. Except for short visits to Scotland, we didn't settle on Robert's estate in Kincardineshire until the spring of 1952. In October he had to go to London on War Office business, so we stayed with Elinor in her flat at Rutland Gate. Like myself, Elinor had become 'a novelist of distinction', as they say.

On the way home I asked my husband to go by the west coast route, so that we could stop in Dumfries for the night and I would, at last, be able to visit Agnes Inglis's home. By this time, Agnes Inglis, unknown to the majority in her lifetime, had become a cult figure. She was sometimes called Scotland's Charlotte Brontë. Volumes of essays about her work, biographies and critical studies were being published every few months. Her letters to Henry James had been published. His to her, of course, had been printed in the 1920 edition of his Letters, edited by Percy Lubbock. Several books about their literary friendship had appeared. The Old Manse, where she had lived for over fifty years, had been turned into a museum with Teenie Peebles, her maid, in charge. 'Dear faithful Teenie, whose devotion to me I can never properly describe,' Agnes Inglis had said in one letter to Henry James; 'Teenie, who to me is nurse, mother, child and stern guardian rolled into one. I could not exist without her. What a treasure she is!'

The treasure was now a dumpy little woman of about seventy, dressed in the style of Queen Victoria, sitting bolt upright on a green velvet chair in the drawing-room. A gawky servant girl with sly black eyes ushered us into the 'presence'. Without waiting for us to introduce ourselves, she said to my husband: 'I am Miss Christine Peebles, who used to be Miss Inglis's companion. I'll be glad to answer any questions you might like to ask. Would you be a professor, sir?'

Robert laughed. 'No, it is my wife who is the professor in our family. My wife is a great admirer of Miss Inglis's books.'

Teenie Peebles gave me the briefest of nods. She knew instinctively that Robert was gentry and I was not. I am not sure how she knew; for on that first pilgrimage I was still young, if you can call thirty-four young, I was still quite pretty and I was very smartly dressed in a costume I'd bought in New York.

'My wife writes books too,' Robert said. 'Novels.'

'I never read novels,' Miss Peebles said. 'I have neither the time nor the inclination. When I was younger, of course, I read all Miss Ness's. She always gave me the manuscript to read before she sent it to her publisher.'

'How wonderful for you,' I said. 'How wonderful to have read *Donna Lucia's Second Husband* and *The Moon Over The Tiber* before anybody else.'

'There was nothing wonderful about it,' she said. 'It was a bit of a trauchle, if you must know the truth. I really didn't have time to pander to Miss Ness and her daftness. I had other things to take up my attention. A house like this doesn't run itself, you know – though maybe you don't, being young.'

I said: 'I manage to run quite a large house.' I was going to add that it was really a castle with well over fifty rooms but, seeing the look in my husband's eye, I desisted.

'She manages to run me successfully, too,' he said. 'Forby finding time to write her books. She's a busy bit lassie.'

Although Teenie Peebles did not actually sniff she implied that she would have sniffed if she hadn't had better manners than either of us. She pushed open a connecting door and ushered us into Agnes Inglis's study.

'Miss Ness spent most of her time in here,' she said. 'When she wasn't sitting at that desk staring into space, she was standing looking out of the window. It wasn't that often she'd be writing when I opened this door. It used to give me a fair scunner sometimes when I saw her empty-handed. "If only ye'd do a bit dusting, Miss Ness," I'd say. "All these knick-knacks and books take such a long time. It would save me, and it'd give you something to do." But she never heeded me. She seemed to forget all the housework I had on my shoulders, forby the cooking in the hinterend.'

'My wife's not a bad cook,' Robert said. 'I'll give her her due. She's a dab hand at scrambled eggs.'

This time Teenie did sniff. 'Miss Ness couldn't even be trusted to boil a kettle. I often said to her: "I'd like to ken what would happen, my lady, if ye were shipwrecked on a desert island. Ye'd never manage to survive." '

'If you don't mind, Miss Peebles,' my husband said, 'I'll go and walk in the garden. I'll leave Lady Dalziel in your good hands.'

While Teenie was showing Robert out, I examined the room that was already familiar from many descriptions by biographers and critics. It was unchanged from Agnes Inglis's time, except for several glass cases in which a selection of her letters and manuscripts were displayed. Some of Henry James's letters were in one case with a card saying they had been found only recently and had not been published yet. I was studying them when a sentence leapt out: 'It is, indeed, I think, the very essence of a good letter to be shown; it is wasted if it is kept for *one* . . . I give you full leave to read mine aloud at your soirées!'

But surely this was not an Inglis letter? Surely he had written it to some other correspondent? Then I realised that James had written it *twice* (perhaps more?) to make sure that one, at least, of his correspondents cherished it for posterity.

'You would be a clever wee girl?' Teenie Peebles said behind me.

I turned and said I supposed I was.

'I was never able to learn my three Rs,' she said. 'I didnie have much chance at the Home. We were all put out to work as soon as we were big enough and strong enough. I was thirteen when I came into Miss Agnes's service. I was an abandoned child.'

I murmured sympathetically.

'Most of the orphans were,' she said. 'I was found on a doorstep in Peebles. They aye cried us after the towns we were found in. That glaikit lassie that showed ye in, Mary Selkirk, she was an abandoned child too. Abandoned in more ways than one. I often wish I had the courage to tell her to pack her bags and get weaving.'

Miss Peebles took a crumpled packet of Woodbines from her cardigan pocket and offered it to me. 'I like a fag now and then,' she said. 'That lassie steals my fags. But what can I say? I need somebody here. I'm ower auld to manage on my lone. I suppose I'll just have to thole her thievin' and her imperence.'

Teenie angrily puffed her cigarette. 'I'm hard put to it whiles not to draw my hand across her lug at the things she says. Especially at what she says ahint my back. She thinks I'm deaf, but I'm no' as deaf as all that. Ach, but I've put up wi' imperence all my life, and I daresay I'll manage to survive a bit more before the Lord calls me.'

She gave another angry puff. 'Miss Ness could be right imperent, too, y'know. She could be a real madam when she took a huff. But I had my own methods o' dealing with her. "Now, Miss Aggie," I'd say. "Enough o' that. We'll have no more of it." She hated being cried Aggie. She was aye cried "Miss Ness", except, like I say, she forgot herself and I had to put her in her place.'

Teenie stubbed out her cigarette. 'It was Miss Ness that taught me to smoke. It was after one of her huffs. She'd had a letter that mornin' from Mr Henry James and somethin' in it had garred her gorge rise. I think it was somethin' about yon Mrs Wharton, a woman Miss Ness and me could never abide. Whatever it was it put Miss Ness in a right paddy, and she was very imperent to me when I brought in her breakfast. I planked down the tray and I said, "Look ye here, Miss Aggie. One mair wrong word frae you and I pack my valise and go." So she laughed then and said: "Och, Teenie, whatever would I do without you? Here, have a cigarette and that will cool you down." Well, I'd never had a smoke, so when she pressed me I indulged for the first time. Many a quiet fag me and Miss Ness had after that when she wanted a wee crack about her writin'.'

Before Teenie had time to reach into her cardigan pocket, I offered her my Gold Flakes. 'I shouldnie chain-smoke,' she said. 'They say it gi'es ye lung cancer. But ach to hang, I'm ower auld to care now.

'It wasn't often that Mr James's letters upset her,' she went on. 'There was aye great excitement when one came. She would sit all mornin' readin' it again and again, and in between whiles she'd stare into vacancy as if she had a want. You'd never have thought to see her then, looking like somebody in a loony-bin, that she was sic a clever woman. Then next day she'd make up her mind to answer it, and she would sit for maybe an hour without havin' written a single word. "What can I say to him, Teenie?" she would say. "He writes such beautiful letters. I feel that mine could never hope to be as good and beautiful as his." So I would say: "Ach, tell him about auld Mattie McLauchlin's white hen that's aye layin' in our hedge", or something like that. Of course she would never write to him about sic daft things. I've often wondered what she did say to Mr James. They tell me her letters to him were printed in a book, but I've never read them.'

I remembered an Agnes Inglis letter to the Master: 'Sitting at this old woodwormed desk, I noticed, looking out of my window, wondering, as I always do, at the beauty of the river valley, which I can glimpse between the tall fir trees, a large bird of dazzling white drifting along beside the hedge, and as I watch this domestic animal (or should it be fowl?), for it turns out to be a hen belonging to a neighbour, I see her disappear into the undergrowth . . .'

I moved over to the window. The branches of a rowan tree tapped against the panes. Beyond it a dark mountain of a monkey-puzzle shut out most of the sky. I could dimly see fir trees behind that, but no sign of the river.

'I see the trees have grown a lot since Miss Inglis died,' I said.

'Och, not that much,' Teenie said. 'The garden's aye been like this – hemmed in by thae big trees.'

'But Miss Inglis has described the view of the river from this window so often,' I protested.

'Havers! We've never been able to see the river from here. She must just have imagined it. She had nothing else to do.'

The door opened suddenly and the servant girl poked her head around it. 'Please, mum, will ye be wantin' tea, Miss Peebles mum?'

'You know fine we'll be wanting tea. I would've thought you'd have had it ready by this time.'

'The kettle's boilin', mum,' Mary Selkirk said. 'But the gentleman – will he be wantin' tea, too, mum? He's sitting in the car.'

'Tell Sir Robert when tea's ready,' I said. 'He'll come quickly enough.'

'Will ye be wantin' biscuits forby the Dundee cake, Miss Peebles mum?'

'Ay, of course, we'll be wantin' biscuits,' Teenie said. 'Bugger off now and bring it in.'

Miss Peebles turned to me with the aplomb that duchesses are supposed to have but often don't. And then she grinned and winked. All pretence was dropped. We were local girls who had made good. She was an abandoned child who'd become châtelaine of a museum; I was a working girl who'd hooked one of the gentry and gotten herself a title.

There was an old fashioned typewriter on a stool beside the desk. 'Did Miss Inglis use that much?' I asked.

'No, she could never be doin' with it. Miss Ness was ower impatient to learn to work it properly. She garred me take lessons on it, though. A lassie in the village came here three nights a week to teach me, but I never made any headway. What was I needin' to type for, anyway! Miss Ness thought of course it would be handy and that she could dictate her stories to me to save herself the hard work of putting pen to paper. But nothing came of that ploy, I'm glad to say.'

The door opened again, and Mary Selkirk looked in. 'There's more folk come to look at the hoose,' she cried. 'What will I say to them, mum? There's no' enough Dundee cake for us all.'

'Tell them the place is shut for the day,' Teenie said. 'Tell them to make an appointment and come another time.'

'Right, mum!' The door banged.

'Really, this place goes like a fair now,' Miss Peebles said, accepting a Gold Flake from my case. 'But when Miss Ness was alive we didn't have so many visitors. She never went anywhere, except maybe once a month for a drive in the carriage to Dumfries. That was when I was still a young woman, mind. As we got older Miss Ness never went over the doorstep.'

'She travelled a lot when she was young,' I said. 'Italy and France and Spain. It was in Italy that she met Henry James. Did you ever go abroad with her?'

'For God's sakes no! She'd done all her travellin' by the time I came here. She was nearly forty and had settled in her groove.'

'Did Mr James ever come here?' I asked.

'No, I never set eyes on hair or hide of him,' Teenie said.

'But that Mrs Wharton **came** once. An American lady. She was chums-a'-bubbly with Mr James. She didn't half put Miss Agnes through the mill. She speired her right, left and centre, asking how she wrote this, why she wrote that, how often she did this, what did she think of that. Puir Miss Ness! Mrs Wharton near enough asked her how often she went to the lavvy.'

'When was this?' I asked.

'Afore the first war, in the days when moty-cars weren't common. Mrs Wharton came in a big one, with her chauffeur, Mr Cook. Such a nice man! Him and me and the other two maids had many a good laugh in the servants' hall at Mrs Wharton and her capers. Now there's nobody to sit in it but that glaikit cratur' Mary Selkirk, who doesn't ken what a good laugh is. Mrs Wharton insisted on taking Miss Ness out in the moty-car for a drive to Ecclefechan to look at a house some auld author was born in. Och, what a palaver there was! Miss Ness had to put on a moty-veil. And Mrs Wharton had on one, too. When they came hame I asked Mr Cook why he didn't wear one, because there was no show without Punch, and he laughed and said: "Miss Peebles, you're a real devil!" Oh, me and Mr Cook got on fine. But yon Mrs Wharton was a different kettle o' fish. Her man was what was called a "neurasthenic" and was in a private hospital. He was really a daftie. His name was Teddy. She was gettin' ready to give him the heave when she was here. Miss Ness was scandalised at the cold-blooded way she talked about him. The poor man didnie ken what a tartar he'd gotten in tow with. He called her "puss". Puss! She was a real scratchy auld cat right enough.'

The door opened and again Mary Selkirk poked her head around it. This time she looked directly at me and said: 'Please yer ladyship, the gentleman – I mean the lord – he's no' in the car. This wee note was lying on the seat.'

The note said: 'Have gone for a walk along the river. Back in one hour. R.'

'That's fine,' said Miss Teenie Peebles. 'We can have a better wee crack without the men-folk. The gentry men dinnie really like tea, anyway. They'd rather have a good glass of the hard stuff.'

'Bring in the tea, lassie,' she said to Mary. 'And bring in the whole Dundee cake. You can get a bit o' what's left. Ye've got plenty o' biscuits in the kitchen to fill ye up.'

She accepted another Gold Flake. 'The General 'll enjoy his wee dander by the river while we enjoy our wee crack,' she said.

'But how did you know he's a general?' I said. 'We never told you.'

'I read the papers, Lady Dalziel, and I've a guid memory for faces. I mind seeing Sir Robert's photygraph in a paper when he saved yon King from bein' killed by some wild Arab heathen.'

Mary Selkirk came in with the tray.

'Now, Lady Dalziel,' Miss Peebles said. 'Will ye have milk in yer tea, or are ye that new-fangled that ye want lemon? If ye want lemon ye'll have to go and look for one.'

'Milk,' I said. 'No sugar.'

'Attagirl!' Teenie said. 'I could never abide sugar in my tea, though it hasnie kept me frae getting fat.'

She handed me a cup, then she nipped out her cigarette, still three-quarters unsmoked, and placed it carefully in the ashtray. 'That'll come in handy later,' she said, giving me a wink. 'Waste not, want not!

'Yon Mrs Wharton!' she exclaimed. 'What a limmer she was! She stayed here for three days, and it felt mair like three weeks. By the end o' it puir Miss Ness was near demented. She had to take to her bed and bide in it for a week after "Puss" left. Puss indeed! She divorced that puir Teddy two three years after that. Miss Ness was more than scandalised. I mind she wrote a long letter about it to Mr James. Oh, she was in a right tizzy!'

I did not know this letter. It was not in their published correspondence, so it looked as though Mr James had not preserved it, probably for his great friend Edith Wharton's sake.

I said: 'It's funny that Miss Inglis never married.'

'What's funny about it?'

'Well, she was a pretty woman,' I said. 'She was a clever woman. In fact, she was a brilliant woman, one of Britain's greatest writers. And I imagine she was a charming woman?'

'Oh, Miss Ness was charming all right. She could charm the backside off a wheelbarrow.' Teenie filled her mouth with Dundee cake, chewed for a few seconds and added: 'But she had no inclination for men.'

'Surprising,' I said. 'She writes so well about them. She understands them completely, and she obviously admired them. Did she never have a great love affair? Did she never talk about some man she'd loved when she was young?'

'The only man she ever talked about was Mr Henry James. Mind you,' Teenie said, taking another large slice of Dundee cake and shoving a good proportion of it into her mouth, 'I aye thought Mr James was a bit of an auld wife. I never met him, but Miss Ness would insist on reading his letters out to me, and I didnie fancy the sound of him. Too much talk! I cannie thole men that talk too much. That was what was wrong with yon imperent young doctor that set his cap at her.'

'What young doctor was this?'

Teenie swallowed the remains of her cake, restrained a belch, wet the tip of her pinkie and mopped up the cake crumbs from her plate.

'Well, he wasn't really as young as all that,' she said. 'He'd be in his middle thirties. But he was cried "the young doctor" to show the difference between him and auld Dr Blackie. His name was Murdie, Dr Thomas Murdie. We aye had Dr Blackie at the Manse, but once when Miss Ness was ailing and there was something wrong with Dr Blackie at the same time the young doctor came instead. There wasn't a great deal wrong with Miss Ness, ye ken, but she got notions into her head that she was ill and dying. Oh, this was when she was about forty-five: I daresay she was near the change o' life. Well, I was young myself then – twenty or so – and I didn't have much time for her aches and pains. But young Dr Murdie played up to her, pampering her as though she was a bairn. He was a well set up man, and I daresay he was good-looking in his way. I didnie fancy him myself, but it wasn't long before I found that Miss Ness did. Foolish cratur' that she was, to be taken in by such a callant! Howsomever, there it was. He was in and out of the house two three times a day. Then, not content with sitting for an hour sometimes, holding her hand and whispering to her, the pair o' them giggling like a couple o' bairns, he took to taking her out in his gig for wee drives. "To blow the cobwebs away," he says to me. "Miss Inglis doesn't get enough fresh air." This was a lot of blethers. Miss Ness had her own carriage and pair if she wanted to go out jaunting, and she could aye get plenty o' air and exercise in the garden. Howsomever, there was nothing I could do about it; I just had to watch her making a fool o' herself. But when he started sending letters I was able to put a spoke in his wheel.'

I held out my Gold Flakes. Teenie glanced at the half-smoked cigarette in the ashtray, pursed her lips and took a fresh one. She lit it and said:

'The doctors employed a half-daft laddie to run their messages, and one day he came with a letter to Miss Ness from Dr Murdie. I opened it. I soon put an end to it at the back o' the kitchen range. The imperence o' the fella to presume that a lady like Miss Ness would even look at him.'

I blew a mouthful of smoke into the air and said: 'Well?'

'It was a note to say he couldn't call for her in the gig at three o'clock, like they'd arranged, but he'd call for her the next day at the same time. I said nothing when Miss Ness got herself all dolled up, with a hat and veil, after lunch and sat in the drawing-room with a book. I kent she expected me to say, "And where are ye off to, Miss Ness?" But I said nothing. Half past two came, three o'clock, half past three and still she was sittin' there with her hat on. The village is two miles away, as ye ken, so naturally she'd never dream o' walking there to meet him. She was never what ye might call a walker, anyway. At four o'clock she went up the stair, and I didnie see her again until six o'clock when she came down and sat at that desk.'

Teenie lifted the teapot and shook it. 'Would ye like another cup?'

I shook my head. 'No, thank you, Miss Peebles.'

'I dinnie think I'll bother either. I dinnie fancy the dregs.' She put the teapot down with a little bang and said: 'Well, the next day I got Miss Ness well out o' the way long before three o'clock. I made some suggestions to her about answering a letter of Mr James's, and she was firmly closeted in here, writing away, when I made it my business to go down the drive and pick some flowers. I was picking away, when Dr Murdie drove up in his gig. I stood just inside the gate so that he couldnie drive his horse in. "Oh, are ye lookin' for Miss Ness, sir?" I said. "She's away to Dumfries for the day. She went early this mornin' with a friend, Mr Henry James, a famous author though ye may no' have heard o' him. I don't expect they'll be back till late. The gentleman's going to bide here for a few days."

'So that was that,' Teenie said. 'He said nothing. He turned his horse and drove away. But the next day the daft laddie came with another note and said he expected an answer. I tellt him the answer would be sent by hand. I burned Dr Murdie's letter after I'd read it – oh, it was that lovey-dovey it near garred me bock! – and then I suggested to Miss Ness she might go to Dumfries in the carriage to buy the new hat she'd been talking about. So off she went, and she wasn't long away before Dr Murdie arrived all in a dither. But he met his match. I tellt him Miss Ness and her friend were away to Lockerbie and they would probably be bidin' the night there. "And who knows?" I said. "Maybe wedding bells will be ringing." For a week on end he sent letters every day, but they all ended up in the kitchen range. Miss Agnes knew nothing about them, so he never got any answers that might have ended up in the *Collected Letters of Agnes Inglis!*'

Teenie laughed and said: 'The upstart, to think he'd be able to hang up his hat with a bonnie, rich lady like Miss Ness! I got a doctor frae Dumfries the next time she thought she was ill, and we had him for a wheen years. In the hinterend, though, we had a lady doctor, and she attended both Miss Ness and me until the end. It was her that made out Miss Ness's death certificate. She died very peacefully, I'm glad to say. She was sitting up in bed eating her breakfast, and she'd just said to me: "There's never anything in the post these mornings, Teenie, there's never been anything worthwhile since poor Mr James died," when she gave a funny wee cry, and lo and behold she was awa' wi' it. I coffined her myself. There was no need for the undertakers. I told them to lay the empty coffin on the bed beside her, after I'd laid her out, and I got a woman friend from the village to help me lift her into it. No man had touched her while she was alive. I was determined no man was going to touch her when she was dead.'

I never saw Teenie Peebles again. I wrote to her, but she never answered. I got Robert to send her a brace of pheasant, and I sent Christmas cards for several years. I always meant to go back to the Old Manse, but I never managed, for when Robert was made Governor of a West Indian island we stayed there for a good many years, and what with this and bringing up two boys and a girl I had time to write only an occasional novel. But now that the children had grown up and had left Robert and me on our own, we were back in Scotland, and made another pilgrimage to the Old Manse.

'What do you mean, madam?' Mary Selkirk said. 'I was never an abandoned child. I still have an old mother alive in Glasgow.'

'But Teenie Peebles told me,' I said. 'She told me . . .'

'Teenie Peebles said a lot more than her prayers,' she said. 'She was a bit of a gabber in her old age. I gather from this that you have been here before?'

'Many years ago,' my husband said.

'Will you please sign the book, sir? And step this way. There is a charge of half a crown for each of you. The money goes to a good cause: The Agnes Inglis Home for Orphan Girls.'

While Robert was signing the visitors' book a girl of about sixteen with long straight fair hair, dressed in tight blue jeans and a crumpled floral blouse, came and leaned against the newel of the stairs. 'Will I make a cuppa, mate?' she asked.

'I don't think so, Dawn,' Mary Selkirk said. 'I don't think the lady and gentleman will be staying that long.'

She glanced at the book: 'Oh, Lord Dalziel!' she exclaimed. 'It isn't often we get such a famous visitor.'

'Don't you remember when we were here before?' I said. 'It's nineteen years ago, but I remember you perfectly.'

'I'm afraid I don't,' she simpered. 'But then, I have a poor memory for names and faces.'

'But you recognised my husband just now.'

'Oh, but that's because he's been so much in the news lately. I've seen him on television. The ceremony about handing that island over to the natives. What was it? Self-government . . .'

'I was in the ceremony too,' I laughed and added: 'But of course, I was done up for the occasion, with false eyelashes and a big lace hat and a mink stole and what-have-you. Mutton done up as lamb!'

'Oh, I wouldn't say that, my lady,' she said.

Mary Selkirk was the kind of woman who would never really be embarrassed, but in case she was, I said: 'Can I see Miss Inglis's study? It's through this door, isn't it?'

Robert said: 'I'll wait in the car, dear.'

The room was the same as I'd remembered it, except that a large photograph of Teenie Peebles, with a permanent wave and a glazed smile, in a silver frame, was on Agnes Inglis's desk in the place where the photograph of Henry James used to be. I walked about the room, peering at the books and the letters in their glass cases, all of them in the same places, and then I found the Henry James photograph half-hidden on the wall at the back of the door.

'I felt it was only right,' said Miss Selkirk behind me, 'that Miss Peebles should take a front place on Agnes Inglis's desk, for after all, it was Teenie Peebles that was the driving force behind her. We must give credit where credit's due.'

'Oh, but Miss Peebles has always been given due recognition in Agnes Inglis's letters and in most of the books written about her,' I said. 'I don't think anybody could ever doubt the important place she had in Agnes Inglis's life.'

'That's as it should be,' Mary Selkirk said. 'It was Miss Peebles that really wrote most of Agnes Inglis's books. Aggie Inglis was a silly woman without a thought in her head. All she was good at was sitting with her head in her hands staring out of that window.'

'But Teenie Peebles was uneducated,' I said. 'I gather she could hardly write her own name.'

'She was far cleverer than she let on,' Miss Selkirk said. 'She gave Aggie Inglis the ideas, and in the long run it was her that dictated the stories and Miss Inglis just wrote them down and put her name to them.'

'But that's nonsense!' I cried. 'I had a great admiration for Miss Peebles, but nothing will make me believe this. She was a totally unlettered woman.'

'Teenie Peebles was a sore trial before she snuffed it,' Miss Selkirk said. 'In fact, she was a cantankerous old bitch, and I had to put up with a lot of her lip when I nursed her in her last days. I have no cause to love her. She treated me very badly when I came here as a young lassie. But over the years she told me all the ins and outs of Agnes Inglis's books, the way they were written, and how this was changed and that was changed when Aggie and Teenie Peebles couldn't agree. And so I'll maintain to my dying day that it was Teenie Peebles who wrote most of Agnes Inglis's books.'

'Well, don't you think it's funny that Miss Peebles never wrote anything in the twenty years after Agnes Inglis's death? It stands to reason that if she was as gifted as you say she was, she would have done something to show it.'

'I remember you now,' Mary Selkirk said. 'I remember you and Teenie drinking tea and eating cake without ever giving a thought to me. You acted like Lady Muck. But I had the size of you. Even if Teenie Peebles hadn't told me afterwards that you came from the Gallowgate in Glasgow, I knew that you were just a jumped-up wee keelie who'd got too big for her boots. I mind what a grand laugh me and Teenie had when you had the cheek to send her a couple of pheasants. I never touched them. I gave my share to the cat.'

'Good afternoon,' I said, walking out.

As I closed the door very gently behind me, I thought: Keep your cool. You're a working class girl who's become a baroness. You must behave like the rest of the gentry. You mustn't lose your rag.

And I thought what a pity it was that Robert had been made only a life peer. I would have liked our oldest boy to be the second Lord Dalziel. Howsomever, as Teenie Peebles would have said, he would be the eleventh baronet. Nothing and nobody could take that away from him, even though, long-haired and bearded as he was (temporarily we hoped), he kept swearing he would renounce the title.

I was sure he would change his mind, and I made up my own that Robert would not send a brace of pheasant to the Old Manse this season.

The girl in the tight jeans was sitting in the back of the car.

'This is Dawn,' Robert said. 'We're giving her a lift to the village.'

'I've got to do some shopping for the auld wife,' she said. 'At the pub, y'know. A bottle of gin. Oh, she'll be well away tonight and I'll have to listen to her life story all over again.'

She leaned back luxuriously and said: 'Smashing car you've got. I'm going to have one like this – only I want a pink one. Yours is too drab a colour.'

'I didn't know that beige was drab,' I said.

'My name's Dawn Hawick,' she said. 'I'm an abandoned child like the rest of them. I was found in a go-cart in

Woolworths in Hawick. My boy friend tells me it's a stigma. But I don't mind. I think it's kinda kinky, don't you?'

I said: 'It's nothing to worry about.'

'Aw, I'm not worried,' she said. 'But auld Selkirk's worried. She thinks it'll keep her out of the next world. Can you imagine! At her age thinking the pearly gates 'll open wide and the Lord God 'll receive her with open arms and say: "Is it you, pet? Come away in." That was all right for Miss Christine Peebles and auld fogies like her, but you'd have thought Mary Selkirk would have more gumption. However, if she believes it, good luck to her!'

She put her elbows on the back of the front seat and leaned over between Robert and me as he manoeuvred the car out of the narrow drive.

'Can I tell you something?' she said. 'It's the biggest laugh of all time. All them books that are supposed to 've been written by Agnes Inglis were really written by Miss Christine Peebles, and she never got a penny for them, nor a bloody thank you. I tell you what it is, missis, it's like it says in the papers: A prophet is without honour in her own country.'

9

NAOMI MITCHISON

THE RED FELLOWS

'AND SO they are giving five pounds a head for the red
fellows! Well, well.' Toddlebonny sank his nose in the glass.
It was likely that he was doing his bit of thinking. Even
today a good old pound note, weary with handling maybe,
but the name of an ancient and reputed Scots Bank over it,
is gey handy in a bar, and five of them would stretch the
best part of a week. And a bar was Toddlebonny's favourite
place. Not that he might not be found among the brackens
at odd times or leaning against a dyke considering. Ploys
came in and out of his mind. It had only been the evening
before that the farmers had decided that if they could all
get together and give a right good-going bonus, they would
get rid of the foxes altogether and be easier in their minds
about the lambs. For the lambing would begin any day now
in the lower fields and the hill ewes a fortnight later. And
why should this good money find its way only into the
pockets of certain ones? Toddlebonny began to think aloud
on this matter, after a look around the bar. For it had become
public knowledge by now.

'I was thinking that Big Willie was getting well above
himself, speaking the way he'd have the money in the
bank!' said a crony of his. He, the same as Toddlebonny, had
been in the merchant navy in the old days, and later on at
the fishing – Cod Eye he was mostly called.

'Ah, keepers! Big Willie MacDonald and they smart visitors in their tweeds and all.'

'Big Willie would be the first to know where the vixens could be, if there were one or two in the plantings. Would you say now, Toddlebonny, that they would pay the five pounds right enough for the young ones? A vixen is a bonny beast, so she is, and a shame to be killing her. She might have thirty pounds inside of her, aye, that she might.'

Toddlebonny considered. 'Aye, now, I was thinking, the schoolmaster was after telling me – oh, a whilie back before any word of all this. Nature, he called it. There was this vixen he had sighted. I'd kept it in mind, for a wee fact will come in handy one day or another. Aye. So if one had a place. Kind of quiet. Like yon old shed of yours at the back. You would hardly be needing it today.'

'Where I have my nets lying.' Cod Eye smiled to himself. 'Aye, aye, a nice soft place is a tangle of old nets.'

'So long as you're not coorying down to the fish hooks!'

'Ah, but I always had a sweet regard for a nice wee bot! And it was never myself on the under side. Sure as you're there, many a pleasant hour – aye, thanks, Toddlebonny, I'll take a wee hauf. But what at all had you in mind?'

'Well, one could make good use of a shed, Cod Eye, though I'm loath to distract you from pleasing memories of torn knickers. We could be doing the thing between us.'

'Aye, so we could. But what thing?'

'Man, are you not hearing me right? The money's the same for the cubs and I know well enough that Big Willie is keeping back a vixen, maybe this one the schoolmaster had a sight of, and why wouldn't he?'

'Aye, so he would if you were him, Toddlebonny. But is a keeper the same made as ourselves?'

'Ah, don't be daft, Cod Eye! We'll need a noose and gloves and a strong sack. And to watch. We must choose our night and go cannily about it. We can't have her strangled and her so useful to us.' They had moved down from the bar now to one of the wee tables. There was nobody listening, nobody at all.

'But if he sees?' Cod Eye whispered into his glass.

'I said watch. And he has his weaknesses.'

'Aye indeed. And one is for my own niece Dugaldina, the one that's in the Glasgow office. And she forever coming down for the weekend. And cleaning! You'd think she wanted to make a hospital out of me.'

'Well now, isn't that the Lord's Providence at work!'

Indeed that was the way it seemed to both of them, and now it was the weekend. Cod Eye had taken his niece Dugaldina with him to the kirk. He himself had been in the choir now for the best part of forty years and his voice was not just what it had been once, but they were a kindly lot and nobody wanting to say a word to hurt him. Dugaldina was getting the dinner ready, for she and her chum Sheila from the same office would need to get the afternoon bus back to Glasgow. 'What's the matter with your wrist, Uncle Dougal?' asked Dugaldina. She hadn't noticed it till just now, but some way it had been a full weekend. This chum of her's, Sheila, had been trying to persuade her to persuade Big Willie to read *Lady Chatterley's Lover* and the both of them in mad giggles, for there was Willie trying to get round Sheila to tell him just what it was about the book that would do him good to read, for he was not that keen on reading. Ach, what a Saturday evening and a nice change from the office! Most weekends when she came, she managed to give her uncle's house a bit clean out, but not this time; she'd barely lifted a brush.

'I'd a bit scrape on a barbed wire,' her uncle said, 'but it's nothing. No, no, you've no need to look, I put plenty on it.' He was fond of the lassie and it had been great the way she and Big Willie had spent the whole evening together, but some way he was wishing she would say goodbye. In case she heard anything. But why should she? They had gone about it cannily and no one to see. The poor beastie had been half strangled, but quick enough with her teeth till they got her tied right. And now she was in the shed with plenty warm bedding and as many soup bones from the butcher's as she could get her teeth into, and soon there'd be wee five pound notes popping out of her.

It was two weekends after and a great feel of spring and scent of flowers and young leaves, and the first lambs crying out for their mothers and the clumsy, clot-fleeced lumps of black-face ewes butting their way through to the right lamb. But Big Willie was in the worst of tempers. Dugaldina couldn't make out at all what was wrong or why he was miscalling the whole glen, for he had not exactly explained to her about the fox bounty nor how that vixen had gone missing. It could have upset a lassie the like of her. Dugaldina had looked forward to a long, sunny Saturday afternoon and into the evening and a certain spot a wee bit up the burn, where you could stare up through the young leaves once you were lying easy there. Ah well, it hadn't gone right. He had seemed – nasty. You felt you couldn't trust him if he had you alone. He'd try and work something off on you. No, she wouldn't go with him in the mood he was in. They had words and she'd gone off saying she was through unless he'd come over and say he was sorry. So she was back early. She came through and there was her uncle and his old crony Toddlebonny unlocking the shed at the end of the garden beyond the blackcurrant and raspberry bushes and the rhubarb. She thought she might as well get a few sticks of rhubarb for the supper; maybe she would get a drop of cream from the farm. See there, the old man hadn't even bothered himself to take out the old raspberry canes!

He was slipping, him. And what at all were they looking at in the shed? She'd just go along. Well! Weren't they the cutest, sweetest, darlingest wee things – 'Uncle Dougal, where did they come from?'

'Quick now! And Toddlebonny was quickest. 'Well now, 'Dina, this is the way it was. We found the poor mother hurt, someone must have had a shot at her so we brought her in – near dead, was she no', Cod Eye? We fed her, for one couldn't let her starve, but neither of us expecting she'd live, and now, see, the bonny wee red fellows she's brought us!'

The vixen flattened her ears, growling, and showed sharp teeth. She was used more or less to Cod Eye and Toddlebonny, but here was a new one and her cubs were not to be touched! Dugaldina moved back quickly: 'What are you going to do with them, Uncle Dougal?'

'Well now, I haven't just thought right, but mind, not a cheep to yon Willie MacDonald. He'd be black angry, two poor old men the like of ourselves taking care of one of his foxes.'

'Aye, that's the God's truth,' said Toddlebonny, 'so you'll not let slip a word?'

'It's not likely I'll be speaking to Willie MacDonald, she said, with a cold kind of look, 'he's none of mine.'

'Never tell me he thinks more of yon Sheila than of yourself!'

'No, it's not that. Not at all.' She looked away at the rhubarb. 'I'm just fed up with him. Let him come and find me if he wants!'

Toddlebonny glanced at Cod Eye; clear as day the two had quarrelled and the one thing they couldn't have was Big Willie coming round after her. 'No, no,' said Cod Eye, 'keep you your pride, lassie. Tell him, just, if he comes smelling after you, that he'll not set foot inside the gate! Aye, that'll fix him.'

She didn't answer. Did she want to unfix him? Men! If she'd had Sheila with her they could have talked it over, but Sheila needed to go and see her folks an odd weekend. She made supper, the old man doing his best to cheer her up talking of the years he'd been in the merchant navy and the ploys he was on in foreign ports, and she wondering all the time how different the stories would have been if he'd been telling them to another man. For indeed there was this hiding and cheating going on half the time and fine if it didn't go too far, but could you count on that? Maybe she'd be best not to think of Big Willie for a while. After all there were boys in the office she could go out with. But some way they hadn't the same feel.

Sure enough, Big Willie came the next day when she was just finished with the Sabbath dinner dishes. He stood at the gate, pressed on the latch, was coming in as though he owned the place! But she went out to meet him and her uncle Dougal watched anxiously from behind the front room curtains. The man had his dog with him and if the dog was to smell – but 'Dina was standing her ground, good lassie! Aye, even with the window shut, he could hear her voice, sharp and angry. He licked his lips. And there, the man was away.

She came back in. 'Uncle Dougal!' she said, 'Willie has told me about the fox bounty and he's accusing you of stealing the vixen and I, Lord forgive me, I said I'd cleaned out the whole place and not a trace of a fox.'

'That's my clever lassie,' he said, 'my good, loyal lassie!'

But didn't she burst into tears: 'I lied to him, I'm as bad as yourself, I'm worse! He'll never – we'll never – go away Uncle Dougal, don't touch me, I've seen through you and I hate you!'

Och the lassies! What is a man to do? If himself had been forty years younger or thirty even, and her not his sister's lassie – but, Lord in Heaven, such thoughts were not seemly! Not a word out of her till bus time and then another month till she came back, this time with her chum, the Sheila lassie. Tight-lipped, she seemed. He had tried to make his peace and listened for a sign of it – aye, there they were giggling away in the top room! 'Did you like what I got for you, hen?' he asked, for she was carrying the big box of chocolates – and, Lord Almighty, the price of it, but there, it came out of the five pounds, his share of the ten! – with yon bonny picture of roses and a pink ribbon. And then the wee bonnet. 'I thought, just, with the bit of tartan and yon feather, you would suit it great!'

'Uncle Dougal,' she said, 'you shouldn't have – you with just your pension! But – ' And here she stopped and looked round at Sheila and made a face. ' – but I suppose it was – '

'Och, not at all,' he said, 'not at all! Aren't you my own good, kind lassie!'

'Well,' she said, 'I'll wear it to the kirk tomorrow, but you'll not mind if I take off the tartan and pin on a piece of material I've got by me. It's just a thought too bright for my costume.'

'Anything at all!' he said, 'And come your ways over to the table. I've these lettuces from my own wee patch and a bit fish, better than you'll get in Glasgow.' He kept wondering, had she said a word to Sheila? Maybe not. Ah, the craft of the creatures!

After their tea, anyway, Sheila went off to pick flowers; there was a carpet, just, in the woods. And Dugaldina said to her uncle: 'Now we'll go and see the red fellows.'

'Ach well – '

'That's what we'll do,' said his niece and gave him a hard look. He got the key and they went down the path past the rhubarb; he unlocked the door. 'There were seven last time,' she said, counting the cubs. Bright-eyed, pretty, soft, making baby growls and pounces.

'Ah well, two of them died, a pure shame it was,' lied Cod Eye. But she did not soften, not at all, just stood looking in a daft kind of way. 'You'll not say a word – ' he began anxiously.

But she shut him up. 'Willie would have killed them just the same as yourself.' They were playing together now, twenty-five pounds worth of wee foxes. She turned her back.

It was a grievous weekend for Cod Eye and no chance of speaking to Toddlebonny until the Monday. But they got together at last. 'Man,' said Toddlebonny, 'what at all has gone wrong?'

'Well, this is it,' said Cod Eye. 'The besom must have watched where I put the key in below the sugar in my blue tin. Aye, she saw and she must have gone out in the night and let them all out. And you and me giving her those sweeties and the bonnet – I wish it might burn her ears off!'

'The wicked, ungrateful lassie! When did you get to know, Cod Eye?'

'Och, just before church time and she and her chum were already down the kirk road and not possible for a thing to be said. But the psalm nigh choked me! And when we were back there was little enough I could say in front of her chum, for they'd the dinner ready and then left together for the bus.'

'Thirty pounds,' said Toddlebonny, shaking his head, 'and all our troubles feeding her, the ungrateful brute, just to skedaddle when the door was opened! Ach, I'm half hoping Big Willie will shoot her, it would serve her right!'

'And me with my wrist bitten and a new lock on my shed and all,' mourned Cod Eye. Sadness fell on them both.

'But I've a notion,' said Toddlebonny, 'surely we might

start breeding dogs? There's the shed and all. If we sold the pups it would be away nicer than killing them.'

'Aye, there's that. If I had not kept my mind steady on the money it would have been beyond me, the poor wee fellows. Pups? If there was a market. But Big Willie is forever getting them off yon Labrador bitch of his – '

'Ah, but the summer visitors will go for wee terriers, half the price to feed. But did she say nothing, the lassie? I can scarcely credit it, and you her own uncle.'

Cod Eye shook his head. 'Ach, all she said was: "cheatery will never thrive" – and her going off to Glasgow with my wee bonnet and the great box of sweeties under her arm!'

10

ROBERT BUCKIE

PENNANT'S TOUR THROUGH SCOTLAND

JIMMY PENNANT pulled back the curtain and gazed down towards the back shed. He just could not resist one more look at his pride and joy.

'Isn't that braw, maw?'

'Aye son, she's a Meeker.'

The bright metal glinted every so often as the sun broke through the puffy clouds which were fairly nipping across the sky.

'Ah think ah'll take hur oot. Jist tae the steeple an' back mibay.'

'As ye say. Bit be awfay careful noo, remember whit yir faither said.'

Jimmy's heart swelled fit to burst as he donned all the special trappings – the helmet, goggles, boots and gauntlets. He wrapped the scarf which bore the colours of his favourite team round his neck and knotted it at the back. It added a bit of colour to the shiny black of the artificial leather.

'Quite the guy,' he thought to himself as he swaggered in front of the mirror on his bedroom door. 'James Dean hud nuthin' oan this.'

He lit one of his last Woodbines and stuck it between his teeth. His eyes narrowed. Hard man. The worst about smoking fags this way was that the hot ash was apt to get in your mouth when they burned down, and this particular brand was finished before you knew where you were. Still, it looked really hard.

His mother watched as he made his way down to the shed with its peeling blue paint and the trellis at the side where it had been hoped that roses would grow.

'He's no' a bad laddie though, a' said an' done.'

Mr Fairlie, the probation officer, would have agreed with this. Jimmy had simply got in with a bad crowd.

'Could happen tae anybody, Mrs Pennant,' he had confided to her over a cup of tea only the other morning.

Her son had persevered for over a year now, saving a bit every week off his hard-earned broo money, helped out every now and then by contributions from the wee brown purse which rarely left his mother's pinny; augmented when the gas man called or when it was time to collect the dividend. She had been in two minds initially, but had finally consented when she saw how determined her boy was.

Jimmy sped off round the corner, leaving her to her motherly dreams.

Later on, at the tea table, the pair of them were fair ettling to say something but remained quiet in the dour light until the father spoke up.

'Well, ah see it's come.'

'Aye. Jimmy's been out already . . .' Mrs Pennant bit her tongue as she caught the full force of her husband's glower.

'Ah thocht ah telt him t' wait.'

It was going to be one of those curious two-sided conversations where three are involved, but Jimmy piped up. 'Oach, Faither, it wiz a' right.'

'Ah've read a loat aboot a' thae accidents.'

'Och! No' wi' this yin, Faither. This is the best thit money kin gi'e ye.'

It was too. Mr Pennant had good connections in the boatyard, and many a night's overtime had gone into producing this fine machine – a geometrical, metallurgical, mechanical masterpiece – a gird, complete with fixed cleek.

Not one of your effete English wooden hoops to be driven with a stick, not one of your ordinary iron girds with a separate bar to make it burl, but a shiny hard steel gird, a perfect circle of superb metal, with a seamless rubber-handled fixed cleek that would drive it with the subtlety and control of a violin bow.

Jimmy and his gird became a familiar sight in the town. Every Wednesday he would race down to the broo, much to the envy of the loafers who helped the brewing industry flourish, and as a consequence had to walk everywhere, and greatly to the consternation of the cashier, who earned not much more than Jimmy, and who had to travel a thrupenny bus fare to get to work. That worked out at half a crown a week. Quite a tidy sum over a year. The cashier was constantly aware of this fact.

He did not like the way Jimmy swaggered in and peeled off just the one glove to sign on the dotted line. He felt Jimmy was making a fool of him. 'Shouldnae be allowed,' he would sometimes blurt out as he stirred his sugary tea in the back-room, even though it was not necessarily in the immediate train of conversation. 'Anybudy that kin afford a gird like that shouldnae get the full benefits. Bloodytwister.'

But it was only a slight twist of fate that had Jimmy standing on the opposite side of the counter.

Since getting his gird, he experienced a new lease in life. He took a keen interest in the world around him now, which he had never done all the time he was at school, and he eventually got to know the history and geography of his immediate region quite well.

Often, in the afternoons, he would take a trip down the docks, right down to the gates, and watch the endless activity about him – a cargo coming in from far-off Sweden, the dredger going out to dump its sludge, cranes squeaking, hammers riveting, cases of whisky smashing . . .

But his favourite journey was to leave the Old Town and travel along the fairly straight and flat road (perfect girding terrain) to Dunmore. You could really bizz along this road especially when you got to the Jewel Carriageway. He often wondered exactly why it was so called, but deduced that this name was given because it was the pride of Scottish highways – certainly there was no other road like it anywhere else that he knew of.

On the way, he passed through Skinflats, where the Pennants could now get their messages thanks to their new-found means of transport.

'See Maw,' he pointed out with justifiable pride, since the Co-op dividend was considerably higher here, 'the gird'll pey fir itsel'.'

Airth was steeped in history. There was a castle where someone had once committed suicide, a mercat cross which was against the law ever to be pulled down, and, as everyone knows, it was the site of the Earth Games. Every year, the complete Pennant clan made two pilgrimages – one to the Earth Games and the other to the Tryst. The menfolk always complained about the Tryst but didn't seem to mind the Games. They always made a bee-line for one of the large tents where the wee yins were not allowed, and seemed quite content to spend the whole afternoon there, even on sunny days. There was always too much hustle and bustle and too many big folk blocking his view for Jimmy actually to see anything of the Games, but there were other attractions: one year he remembered having his photograph taken and seeing it being developed right there on the spot. It was small and very dark, but if you looked closely, there was no mistaking the outlines of the young James Pennant.

Not much farther, by gird anyway, was the tiny village of Dunmore. It had a magical character, reminding Jimmy of the pictures in some books he had seen when he was a very small boy.

Flanking a central green, in the middle of which was an antiquated hand-pump, were two rows of unusual little houses. They were stone built and had wizened creepers spread flat all over, giving their faces the dried-out, weather-broken appearance that old men have. There was the tiniest of post offices with a faded red VR letterbox outside, but the most curious was the blacksmith's workshop. The hewn stone arched round the doorway in the shape of a gigantic horseshoe.

At the far end of the green was a tiny landing stage with steps leading right into the Forth. This provided a mooring place for but the smallest of craft, but in time long gone past it had been a great port – some say the largest in Scotland – which saw vigorous trading and fierce battling. In evidence, the wooden ribs of various hulks could be seen poking through the mud here and there, like great carcasses left out to rot.

There was more yet to be seen in the vicinity of Dunmore. He would plank his gird carefully in the long grass beside the hedge so that only he knew where it was hidden, then follow the path deep into the Estate, ignoring the sign which declared, 'Trespassers will be prosecuted.'

There, boldly in front of him, carved entirely from stone, and in the shape of the fruit depicted on the cans that his mother bought, was a gigantic pineapple. He beat his way through and investigated. It consisted of one room, but beneath this were two others from which corridors led off along the full breadth of the garden-jungle.

After this first confrontation he had raced down to the local library to find out more. Though his knowledge was generally derived from the spoken word, he occasionally had to resort to the written when the time span involved was far beyond the ken of his elders.

He discovered that the house had been built by one of the Earls of Dunmore so that he could grow – yes – pineapples.

'Imagine that, noo,' thought Jimmy in wonderment. 'Pineapples in Scoatland, an' hundrids o' years ago tae.'

One day during the summer, Jimmy suddenly announced that he was going on a tour of Scotland.

'An' whaur di ye think ye'll go, ma wee son?' inquired his mother, ever fretful of her boy.

'Ah've worked it a' oot. Ah goat a map frae the garige and ah've drawn owre the roads heavy the yins that'll take.'

It was a map of Central Scotland which overlapped parts of East, West, North and South. If all the parts were brought together it would form a complete mosaic of the land (as depicted on the small map on the back cover), and would probably cover the whole of the scullery floor. It let him see how large the country really was. He had outlined his itinerary, a rough oval shape, with the broad carpenter's pencil which was kept in the kitchen drawer next to the knives.

'See. Ah'll cut acroass at the Kincairdin' Brig and stoap at Cooruss.' Why it was ever spelled 'Culross' was beyond Jimmy. He had seen the single decker pass by twice a day for many years with the sign 'Culross' on the indicators before it dawned on him that it was in fact, the bus to Cooruss. 'Then ah'll gang tae Dumfermlin' an' then head back tae the ferry at Rosyth. Frae Queensferry,' he explained as he traced the route with his stubby forefinger, 'ah'll cut through Linlithgow an' Boneyucks then back hame. Ah'll be awa' quite a while – twa or three days ah think.'

'Oh Jimmy, are ye shair? Hud ye no' be'er speak tae yir faithir first? It's an awfy trek awa' oot there on yir ain.'

Jimmy screwed up his face in filial exasperation.

'Och awa'. Ah'm grouen up noo maw. Ah'll be OK. Ah've goat a len o' a tent frae wee Eleck Rutherford an' ah've been keeping a wee bit back iviry week instead i' gawin' tae the picturs or the gemme. Ah think ah'll leave first thing efter the broo oan Wednesday moarnin'.'

Mr Pennant had mixed feelings but showed no expression. He was now against the gird because it irked him to think that his son was tearing about all over the place while he had to sweat as usual to keep the family in bread and butter, yet, at the same time, he was secretly glad that his son could and did own such a fine piece of craftsmanship. It was the Rolls-Royce of girds in his eyes. He was worried about Jimmy, him going off so far on his own and for such a long time – all sorts of things could happen, and did, in his newspaper-fed imagination – but on the other hand he was glad to see certain signs of manhood in this independence and adventure. He merely muttered something which his wife took to be 'Oh aye', and his son thought was a long sigh, and returned to his sports page and mince and tatties.

The big moment took ages to come, but come it eventually did. Jimmy's mother kissed him on the cheek just before he left. These days it was an embarrassment but he would thole it this once because he sensed what she felt. He adjusted the pack on his back and stuffed the brown poke of corned-beef pieces into his pocket. A final check that he had his map, his money, his cigarettes; a quick wipe to remove the dirt from his gird, and he was off.

He was soon to be seen wheeching down the familiar stretch which led to the roundabout. Instead of going straight on as if going to Airth, he turned right this time and made for the bridge. It was the biggest bridge of its kind in the world. He had heard it said, actually, that most of the bridges over the Forth were the biggest of their kind in the world. Certainly, the Forth Bridge was, for he had never seen a picture of another bridge that anywhere touched it. No wonder the Germans had orders to blow it up first thing during the War.

Culross reminded him in a way of Dunmore, with Airth Castle and the Mercat Cross mixed in. Some of the houses were similar to the ones in a book his mother used to read to him when he was a bairn, cuddled up ready for bed, about a dragon who lived on top of a mountain and who could not stop crying. The dragon's tears rolled down to the town below and began to flood the streets. Many of the houses in the pictures had crooked walls and jutted out the higher they went, just like here in Culross. He couldn't remember how they stopped the dragon crying, but no one was drowned and they all lived happily ever after.

He blessed the fact that he had a gird, for there was no problem in manoeuvring through the narrow cobbled streets. The single decker could never get past. It would have to turn at the bottom no doubt, and the passengers would have to alight and pant and wheeze their way up if they wanted to see the Abbey or the House with the Evil Eyes. Why did they use single deckers anyway, Jimmy wondered – there were no low bridges.

The road to Dunfermline was more up and down. It tested the roadworthiness of the gird to its limits, and proud to say, it passed with flying colours. He decided to pitch camp a good few miles out of town and make his way in in the morning. Jimmy was no stranger to camping. Once or twice he and Eleck Rutherford had gone across the other side of the Carron to what was called the Island, and had spent the night out, returning home as soon as the bitter morning chill woke them up and set their teeth chittering. He felt quite prepared to spend two or even three nights in the rough.

The tent was soon erected and since that was all that had to be done, he produced from the side pocket of his pack a copy of the *Sunday Post* and began to smooth it out. He had managed to refrain from reading it on Sunday, apart from the front and back pages which he just had to keek at. What more could anyone ask for in life: a good read, a wholesome meal of lemonade, chocolate and crisps, followed by the pleasure of a good smoke and cough, while sitting by a burn in front of your tent as the sun was going down. His head was dizzy with the thought of it. He was no longer James Dean, but a Scots warrior of hundreds of years ago. He would have liked fine to have been wearing the kilt at that very moment and be able to swagger into Dunfermline Toon in the morning.

It was a pity that wee Eleck could not be with him to share his great adventure, but as he did not have a gird, he would be hard put to trying to keep up with Jimmy. He and Jimmy had been boon companions in thick and thin; sat together in school and stood together in court.

Neither could give a reasonable explanation that fateful day, but to tell would have been to break a sacred oath. The pair of them had been initiated a few months previously in Smithy's coal shed as members of his gang. Besides the fire and water ritual, which entailed holding the palm of the hand over a burning candle without yelping, and drinking a foul mixture of peeings and lemonade without retching, they had to supply each member of the gang with a wallet and a diary.

It was very hard to hide five wallets and five diaries in their pockets and even harder to explain them away when they were inevitably caught. The store manager found a sympathetic ear when he took them down to the police station.

'It's no' really the money. Ye see, yince they get started they dinnae ken when tae stoap. Ah think they should learn their lesson the noo an' save them a loat o' trouble la'er oan.'

'Ah'm wi' ye there. One hundrid per cent. We ken this pair frae a long time. Broke auld Leishman's windae and pinched her rhubarb, an' swore a' hur tae.'

Jimmy and Eleck blushed violently: their sins had found them out.

Probation wasn't too bad though. It gave his mother a chance for a wee blether with Mr Fairlie now and then.

The morning, unfortunately was not so rosy. It was drizzling when he woke up – finally woke up – for he seemed to have awakened about fifty times during the night. The ground had grown harder and harder while the blankets had grown damper and damper. He had taken the *Sunday Post* and spread it over him according to the well-known practice of tramps, but he was not certain whether tramps lay on top of the papers or laid the papers on top of them. Jimmy did both, and to be on the safe side, covered his legs with the map of Central Scotland.

The cramp was gone but he was still soaked to the skin as he parked his gird behind the café door. He chose the seat by the window so that he could keep an eye on the gird and also watch the world go by. His cigarettes had got soaked during the evening and tasted vile, but he persevered while waiting for the waitress to bring him his breakfast. He was ravenous.

It was obviously not going to be his day. He had to wait for ages. The ham was burned hard. The egg must have been laid by a sparrow. He lost a penny in the Beechnut machine when he was supposed to get two packets. It was drizzling steady. He had left his Pac-a-mac at home. And this was his holidays too.

As he was not in a mood to go his gird that morning, he slung it over his shoulder and wandered dejectedly into the centre of the town until he came to a sub-post office.

'Having a smashing time. Weather not too bad. Love Jimmy,' was the consoling message he wrote on the post-card. He had to squeeze 'Mr &' in front of 'Mrs Pennant' when he read the address he had written, as he would not like his father to feel left out. There was no need for him to have brought the pencil. He had forgotten about the pens chained up beside the little boxes with the green forms. It seemed more proper, and legal too probably, to write in ink, even though he usually made at least one blot when he did.

'Whit is thir tae see in Dumfermlin', Misses?' he asked the woman behind the counter. She reminded him somewhat of a budgie. Her vocabulary reinforced this impression.

'Eh?'

'Ah've nivir been here afore an' ah wiz wunderin' whit thir is tae see.'

'Aw.'

She had obviously never encountered tourists before.

He was not interested in any of the buildings that she had suggested visiting, and opted for the Glen, but it proved hard to negotiate the paths made slippy by the constant drizzle, so he decided he might as well make his way to the crossing at the Forth. In one way, Dunfermline was not a disappointment: the buses in Fife were red, in contrast to Stirlingshire's blue, which gave the town a distinctly foreign atmosphere.

Jimmy's tour was the focal point of conversation while he was away.

'How's the boay, Mrs Pennant?' asked Meikle the Grocer's.

'Aw, he's jist fine. Goat a postcaird frae him thi s'moarning,' she lied in self-reassurement. 'He's hae'in' a great time an' the weather's no' sae bad either.'

'Ay, it's guid fir a laddie tae dae whit he's daein'. Wiz that half a pound ye said?'

'Aye,' she lied again.

Over their morning cuppa, Wee Jeannie, the landing's Job's Comforter, inquired:

'Ur ye no' awfae feart, Nessie? Did ye no' see aboot that young fella that wiz foond deed in the papers.'

'Och, oor Jimmy kin fend fir hissel'.'

'Aye. They say the attack wiz brutil. They think it wiz the work o' a maniac.'

'Ur ye fir another cup, Jean?'

'Jist half a cup Nessie – ah'll hae tae scoot afore Wullie comes in. Shows ye though, ye cannae bide awa' frae yir back-step thae days.'

This was all Mrs Pennant needed to help get through her sleepless nights.

He was lucky to catch the ferry without a long wait, but there was some trouble deciding an appropriate charge for transporting the gird. They wanted to charge the same as for a motorbike until Jimmy pointed out that as a gird had only one wheel the charge should be half that. They finally compromised by charging the same rate as an ordinary pushbike.

The damp, depressing drizzle lessened to a microscopic mizzle until it was held in such fine suspension that it had ceased to fall at all, but just hung there, permeating everything, worse than a downpour.

The crossing was quite a memorable experience. He had once been on one of the tugs in the docks as far as the Swing Bridge, but here you really got the feeling of being at open sea as the courageous little Queen ploughed up and down through the watery furrows. From this vantage point, the bridge looked colossal.

'Ye ken it takes three full years tae pent the brig, and yince that's din they've goat tae start a' ower again cause it's a' rusty.'

A knowledgeable fellow passenger had struck up a conversation.

'So ah've heard,' replied Jimmy. 'A bloke yince telt me there's a fortune tae be picked up frae a' the folk throwin' money oot o' the train windaes. Ye wid think they wid send a diver doon.'

'Aye, so ye wid. See yon hoose?' he pointed as they approached the south shore. 'That's whit ye ca' the Hawes Inn. That's whaur Sir Walter Scott and Robert Louis Stevenson wrote a loat o' their books. Ye see, there wiz a loat o' smugglers in they days.'

'Aye, they wir the days,' Jimmy replied wistfully. 'They mustae hud a great time.'

Although his reading habits stretched little further than comics or the opening pages of a few paperbacks, he was well acquainted with the two writers mentioned, being the authors of *Ivanhoe* and *Dr Jekyll and Mr Hyde*, both films which he had seen.

On arrival, he felt fair wabbit, so he made his way to a small café where he could sit down and dry out. He had a welcome tea of fried eggs, beans and chips, with slices of bread and doubtful butter to mop up the yellow and brown liquid residue.

The waitress in the tight black satiny uniform which made her bulge out in the most unnatural places, totted up the bill and handed him the change from a ten shilling note. This left him with very little, since he also bought ten cigarettes, and, on impulse, a roll of Polos and a packet of chewing gum.

He would pitch camp somewhere on the far side of town for the evening and continue with his great expedition the next day, hoping to arrive home in time for his tea.

Queensferry was an unusual place. There was really only one street and no cinema. There was a curious place called the Church of Mount Carmel. As he made his way out along the shore road, he thought up jokes about this church, really funny ones, which he hoped he could remember so he could tell his parents.

'Nivir mind, wee son,' Mrs Pennant tried to console her boy, 'tell yir faithir the night when he comes in an' ye can see the poalis the moarn.'

Jimmy was only a kick off being heartbroken.

'It wiznae till ah wiz a' ready tae go that ah noticed it wiz away. Ah searched a' roond the place bit thir wiz nuchin' there.'

When the sad tale was recounted later that evening to the head of the household, the response was as noncommittal as ever.

'It's no' jist the gird, Peter, they hud taken a' the chainge tae oot o' his trooser poackets. Ye should hae seen that laddie's feet – ay wiz hirplin' by the time ay goat up the stairs.'

She pulled Jimmy's head into her bountiful side and stroked his hair affectionately.

'Pair wee sowel, hivin' tae walk a' that wey hame.'

That summer saw many changes. Gone were the adolescent pimples from his face, for his travels had made a man of him; gone was the boyhood Gang, for he now belonged to a factory fraternity. Gone, of course, was the gird (the police never did find any trace of it) followed not long afterwards by Auld Sanny, its prime architect and constructor, when he slid peacefully down that Great Slipway, taking his secret with him.

But worst of all for Jimmy, gone was the prestige and luxury of owning a gird: he would just have to walk, like everyone else.

GILES GORDON

DOLORES

THEY were drinking in a bar, one of the village's few. They had not known each other before. Each had ordered a drink, separately. Diogenes first, then Manhattan. 'One whisky and water.' 'One whisky sour.' They'd glanced sideways at each other along the bar, before they'd spoken. After that they hardly looked at each other. 'Another whisky and water.' 'Another whisky sour.' They lost their initial shyness of one another after an hour – not less. At first there had been few words, little more than grunts, acknowledgments of an awareness of the other. Casual, inconsequential phrases. Then one of them said something more private, more intimate. Then the other. Maybe the one's openness encouraged the other. Then they were confiding in one another as old friends.

A start, a building. A residence that shelters people, the inhabitants of it. There is a roof over their heads, there are walls that keep them dry, that should keep them warm. If there is more than one person in the house at night, they snuggle together, touch each other in bed, when sleeping in the same bed. Breathe the same air, breathe in each other's direction.

'Where are we? Where is the picture in your mind?' No answer. The other man stared into his glass. 'Here?'

A house by the sea, somewhere. Blue waves – picture book waves – lapping the shore, softly caressing the beach. Nothing unromantic, nothing histrionic or rhetorical. Sun pours down on to the house, scorches the tiles. Like a searchlight, the sun's rays encompass the house, inside and outside; the patio, the bodies browning themselves.

He smiled, shrugged his shoulders. The other man persisted with his question.

'South of France?'

'South of anywhere.'

'But the location is . . .'

'Important?'

'Well, yes. It is, isn't it? The weather, the climate. If it is hot – really hot – people's tempers . . . It explains a great deal.'

'There is this house. It is . . . in a hot country. Hotter than here, at any rate.'

'But it's only March!'

'Not too far from the equator. The walls of the houses, the streets, are orange, sun baked, sun cracked. Sepia.'

'Ah, Italy?'

'Not . . . necessarily. I refuse to be specific in the location. Not necessary. Detracts from the people. Though the girl, Dolores –'

'Spanish?'

'No, no, no. Or maybe. Perhaps. Possibly. No. You are asking the wrong *kind* of questions. She must not be confined to one country. She was not.' A pause, then: 'Dolores . . .'

'Her name. I accept that.'

'I am not disguising it.'

'She visited the house?'

'No!'

'She lived in it?'

'I'm sorry. Again you are trying to pre-empt my conclusion. I must proceed at my own speed, otherwise I cannot convey the nuances of meaning I need to convey, boring though they may be to you. There is no other way I can tell the tale.'

Manhattan bowed his head, mock humbly; said nothing in reply. Waited for Diogenes to continue.

'A shell of a house. You can see it a mile away, on the winding road from the mountain down to the village. The first thing you notice is that half the roof is intact. That, rather than that half is missing. The condition of the house makes it curious that some of the roof still affords protection. In the harbour, four, five, sometimes there are six fishing boats. Not pleasure boats: the villagers, some of them, make their living from these boats. Sometimes unloading boxes of packed, iced fish; lorries waiting. Gulls circling, cackling above. Making circles, arcs round the masts. You look up from the harbour, from the pier. Along the coast a little, an inch or so below eye level as you look, half a mile away. The house is out of the village, separated from the other buildings by two fields – one rich green, sprouting with shoots; the other brown, furrowed, the earth turned over, the sub-soil parched by the sun – and hedges and waste-land. You can't proceed from the village or the harbour through the fields to the house, not legally and certainly not easily.'

'The house is isolated. No one lives in it?'

'You know that?'

Manhattan smiled: 'I seek information.'

Diogenes looked quizzical, then continued after a sip at his drink.

'Officially, no one has lived there for decades. For a hundred years, perhaps. The road that was there – if there was a road; there *must* have been a road – is overgrown, choked with greenery, dykes, hedges, roots, ditches, even barbed wire where you least expect it. The only route is along the shore, by the sea and scrambling up eight feet when the gardens of the house, which lead down to the sea, are reached. Not that easy. You have to be agile.'

'You've done it?' ventured Manhattan. Diogenes smiled.

'That would be telling. That would be giving away more than at this stage I'm prepared to tell you, or anyone.'

'Cautious,' said Manhattan. 'Yet by saying as much as you have I know what I know.'

'You think so?' said Diogenes.

'I think so,' said Manhattan, circling Diogenes in conversation as Diogenes was circling him, and as Diogenes was circling himself. Whether these two men were unhappy, neither was yet – if at all – prepared to reveal to the other. It was one thing to confide, another to confess.

Manhattan offered Diogenes a drink. Diogenes, not ungrateful, asked for a whisky sour. Manhattan had a whisky and water. The barman accepted without thinking about it that these two customers did not at this time want to chat to him, to inquire as to the basic amenities of the area, assuming he and they had more than the rudiments of a language in common. Maybe one of them would ask about the local life when the other had departed, assuming they didn't leave together.

Manhattan looked at Diogenes: 'Tell me about her.'

Diogenes looked at Manhattan: 'Mmm?'

'You must be telling me this because it is about a woman. You said her name was Dolores.'

Diogenes smiled. 'How old are you?'

'I should know better. Forty-seven.'

'I'm forty-six.'

'Married?'

'I have a wife.'

'Here? With you?'

'Elsewhere.'

'And me.'

A little silence, each of them perhaps thinking of his wife, or of other women. Then Diogenes began to talk quickly.

'Inside the building, on the first floor, was a statue. I thought it was a woman. It was so beautiful, and elusive, classical. I've never reacted so . . . to a statue. I don't go around being influenced by statues! Its face, features, cheekbones – oh, the cheekbones! – the mouth, the eyes. They drew me through them, they drew me through them, through the eye sockets, so it seemed. And not all the floorboards were there so I had to be very careful, had to keep looking down at my feet. The nose was ordinary, but I didn't see that till afterwards. I should have suspected the nose. But it wasn't an objective situation, you can see that, can't you?'

Manhattan didn't respond, didn't look at Diogenes. He was buried in his own thoughts. Diogenes focused back on his memory.

'It was near the window, the statue; the large, horizontal window. The statue, if placed in such a position, at the right angle, gazed out to sea. But it was facing into the room, the back of its head to sea. There was nothing else in the room. Nothing. Not when I saw it. Not a table, not a chair, not even a sheet of paper or an empty matchbox. Which was why it took me by surprise, perhaps. Perhaps that was it. I was, well, confronted with it. The statue was clothed.'

'Clothed?'

Manhattan frowned, trying to grasp the picture in his mind.

'Not in a suit. I don't mean anything like that.'

'But it was a bust? A head?'

'It had a torso. I thought it had, at any rate.'

'I hadn't seen it that way. I was imagining it as a head.'

'There was the head – I've told you about the head – and the neck. The neck was slender, elegantly shaped, magnificent. What can you say about a neck? Then there were the shoulders. Or I thought there were. There should have been.'

'If there was a body, there must have been shoulders.'

Diogenes seemed to consider this. He poured a little water into his glass, either to make the drink last longer or to dilute it. Then he continued, as if the intensity of the experience was too great for him to convey it remotely in words.

'Its torso, what I thought was its torso, was draped with a cloth, a robe, a cloak. Maroon. Crimson. Almost an oyster purple, but red. Rusty with blood colour, smeared with dry red clay colour. In no time the colour changed, kaleido-scopically. The light flooding through the vast window, you understand? I don't know what colour the sheet was – orange, probably.' He took another sip at his drink. 'I thought it was a robe, a garment, until I touched it. Why did I touch it? Oh, possession, possession. Anyway, it was wet. When I held it in my hands it was soaking.'

Diogenes was perspiring, and he clenched and unclenched his hands as if at that moment he was holding, then releasing the wet cloth.

'Soaking?' asked Manhattan, not understanding.

'No, I exaggerate. Not soaking. But wet, very wet. Damp. And when I looked down at my fingers they were red. My God, she's dying, I thought, and looked round the room hoping no one was there, that no one had crept in after me, witnessed the deed. Then I realised she wasn't moving. My God, she's dead already, I thought, and looked at the shoulders I'd revealed by ripping off the cloak. Then I hoped that someone *had* witnessed the deed, they would know that I had committed no crime, committed at least no murder. My hands were red, sticky, the red would dry on me. The day was very hot. I held the damp cloth. The dye was coming off the cloth, the colour was not from the statue. The cloth had been to keep the clay moist, the body was not yet complete. I held the cloth. I dropped the cloth. I can't remember where I put it, after the initial shock had subsided.'

He paused, indeed stopped. It was as if he couldn't go on, so confounded was he by his own revelations. Manhattan didn't wonder why Diogenes was telling him – had told him – these things, but he couldn't immediately understand what relevance they had to his life, how they related to his own experience.

There were more people in the bar now, ten or twelve. Diogenes and Manhattan were vaguely aware of the newcomers, though they couldn't have said how many there were. Diogenes moved along the bar a little, so that he could lean his face towards Manhattan's.

'It had no tits, my friend. It had a flat chest, no nipples. It was a bloody man. No privates because it ended way above where they would have been, above the waist. A man! You can imagine how embarrassed I was. Anyone might have seen, had there been anyone there, had the room, the house been in a public thoroughfare.'

Diogenes cleared his throat, punched the glass along the bar on which he leaned, then drew it back towards him. He pushed it backwards and forwards, from palm to palm. There was no liquid left in it, only a drop or two.

Manhattan realised he had to say something, but he knew that his companion would not expect him to say what he was going to say.

'I don't see why . . . ? A statue . . . ?'

'But, don't you see, I had thought it a woman. Its face, I fell for it. Loved it, if you like. I wanted it to be a woman.'

'But no one saw you.'

143

Diogenes knew he would say that, in a reassuring way. He was prepared for the remark.

'No one saw me – at first. There was only the statue, facing into the room, looking at me when it should have been looking out to sea. Wherever I moved in the room, to try to avoid its eyes, as long as I was in front of it it kept its eyes on me. I knew what I had done, the thoughts I had been having. It *accused* me, without saying a word. It didn't have to speak. I was still holding its drape, whatever it was. That made it worse. I didn't want the blasted thing, not if it belonged to a man. It was a sweltering day, I hardly needed it to keep me warm. I wanted to be rid of it.'

Manhattan was now only half listening. His mind was coursing down other channels of thought, started by Diogenes' story.

'Why didn't you put it back on the statue's shoulders?' said Manhattan.

'Had I done that, it would have been a woman again. At least it would have looked like a woman. I didn't want it to look like a woman when it was a man.'

'But a statue . . . ?'

'Not to me. Not to me. Not just a statue, not any old statue.' He reflected upon something before continuing. 'And what was it doing there? In a large, empty room in a large derelict house above the sea, magnificently sited? The statue three feet or so from the window, from the glass. The glass was burning hot, too. I touched it at one point. When I stood between the window and the statue I still felt those eyes boring into my skull. They seemed to burn directly into my eyes when I stood between the sea and the back of the statue's head.'

'So the glass was a mirror?'

Diogenes looked puzzled, as if trying to interpret what Manhattan was saying.

144

'No, not a mirror. If so, the sea was the statue's face, and that wasn't how it was at all. If anything, I was a mirror, between the sea and the face, between the head and the glass. I was still holding that cloak – whatever it was – when I heard a sound to my left. I was aware of a sudden movement, the creaking of a floorboard. I looked along the floor, keeping my eyes down for some reason. For no particular reason. There was a woman standing there. Well inside the room, ten paces from the door. I hadn't seen her come in, I hadn't heard her. I'm sure she wasn't in the house when I entered, and climbed the wide staircase.'

Diogenes again stopped abruptly. Manhattan turned to look at him. He was sweating profusely now. Though the day was hot enough, the bar was cool, shaded. Diogenes had turned pale. His thick, dry lips were moving up and down with rapidity, as if he was silently telling a rosary.

'Here, my dear chap,' said Manhattan, 'have another whisky.'

Diogenes gave no indication of having heard what Manhattan said. Manhattan gesticulated to the barman, who had been chatting with a group of men at the other end of the bar. He took away their glasses, replaced them with new drinks.

'A woman, you say?' said Manhattan.

Diogenes spoke again, as if in a trance. His voice had lost its resonance, its fluidity of expression.

'She walked towards me. She must have done. I didn't see her move, and I thought I was looking at her all the time, but she was beside me. Standing next to me. How had she crossed the room – a large room, twenty or thirty feet between us – without my noticing? If I went back to the house now, to that room, I couldn't say: she stood *there*; *that* was the door she came through. Which is strange, as there is no doubt in my mind as to where the statue was.'

He took a gulp at his glass, without giving any indication that he realised he was drinking. 'She took the cloak, cloth – whatever it was – from my hands. She snatched it away, without touching my fingers with hers, without coming into contact with my body. It was in my hands, then I didn't hold it. She wrapped it round the shoulders of the statue, the sculpture, precisely as it had been before I removed it. What was odd was that as soon as I saw it on the statue again I couldn't be certain that I had ever held the garment. It seemed not to have been moved. The folds, the angles were as they had first been, yet she had achieved them without attempting to recreate the original position. She – the statue; it – was a woman again, beautiful as before, the same as before.'

Manhattan, his concentration again having lapsed, wondered how many times Diogenes had narrated this story. Had it happened, could it have happened? Had it more credibility as a fiction, or as reality? Diogenes had not reached his conclusion yet.

'I gazed once again into those eyes. They stared back, entrancing me, hypnotising me. The eyes were . . . familiar. I had seen them somewhere, and not just in the statue. Where, where? My mind worried at the problem as I kept staring at them, knowing that eventually the connection would become apparent. A thought occurred. I had forgotten the woman, her presence. She who had withdrawn the cloak from me, dressed the statue again. She who had made me a second time think of the face as female. I looked round, to where she was standing, where she had been standing.'

'She wasn't there.'

'You knew? How?'

'It was obvious that that was what you were telling me, what you were leading to.'

146

'Obvious?'

'Yes, I think so.'

'You've heard the story before?'

'Not at all. At least –' and here Manhattan smiled at Diogenes ' – if I have I don't remember a word of it.'

'You don't believe me?'

'Oh, I believe you.'

'Well, then . . . ?'

'She was a sculptress. Her name was Dolores.'

'Her name was not Dolores.'

'Whatever it was. She was a sculptress, making a statue in her own image.'

'Why? If you are correct, why? Why should anyone want to do that?'

'There are reasons. We know that.'

'Do you think the reasons matter?'

'It depends what interpretation is placed upon them. It mattered to her. Though she could not live in the house, maybe she wanted something of her to be there, to remain?'

'Maybe. Perhaps she found stones on the beach to thrust in the eyes?'

'Glass, more likely, if you thought the eyes were her own.'

'They stared at me. They never blinked, never closed. They were at it all the time, looking, assessing.'

'The flesh over glass eyes can fold and unfold, blink, unblink. The eyelids come down. And rise up.'

'There was no flesh in this statue.'

'I know! You called the statue Dolores.'

'No. I never thought of it as possessing a name.'

'To be nameless is to have an identity.'

'She had ceased to be flesh. She was . . . petrified.'

'You said it was a man. You seemed, a few minutes ago, appalled by that.'

'Appalled? No. I was, I admit, a little overcome, at the time. It was a shock. It wasn't what I expected.'

'But were the subsequent occurrences?'

'I looked from the eyes of the statue to where she had been. I drew my eyes back, somehow caught sight of my hands. They were red, sticky. It wasn't clay, it wasn't paint, it wasn't dye.'

There was only one other substance it could have been, Manhattan realised, but he wasn't prepared to play entirely into the hands of Diogenes. He was listening to what he had to say, he was indulging his story-telling. Was that not enough? Diogenes should be made to work. His audience should be sceptical for the narration to have a fine edge. Manhattan raised his glass to his lips, again dry, and sipped. Diogenes realised he was going to say nothing.

'I knew where she was.'

'The sculptress?'

'Yes. In another room in the house. She was tempting me, encouraging me. Leading me on.'

'Not . . . warning you?'

'Of what?' Diogenes looked puzzled, and taken aback. This was an angle he had not considered, though he realised immediately that it was consistent with the facts as he had revealed them.

'Oh, I don't know. A thought, that was all.'

'I was prepared to be tempted – up to a point. To what point had to be seen. But I was game to play her game, if she was playing a game. And I was sure she was. The house was isolated. It was impossible that anyone could hear anything, if we talked, if anything – unforeseen – happened.'

'Not impossible. Improbable.'

'You're very pedantic.'

'Not at all. If you found your way to the house, and

indeed if the sculptress did, you might have been followed in your turn.'

Diogenes glanced round at Manhattan, for the first time as if suspicious of something, as if Manhattan was making deductions from what he was saying.

'I looked at the statue again. It looked at me. It knew about my red hands, I could tell that. Its eyes were inscrutable.'

Diogenes seemed to falter, as if not to know how to continue; as if Manhattan's remarks worried him, made him not wish to conclude.

'It had just been made by the sculptress. Its head,' said Manhattan. 'Its body hadn't been completed yet, hence the unformed torso, hence the wet cloth keeping the clay damp, hence the redness on your hands.'

'You think so? Logically, yes. But how do you explain the expression in the eyes, the experience, the *knowledge* that face possessed? Nothing could surprise that head. Classical in feature, it spanned the centuries in awareness. Its back to the sea, it grew out of the ocean, it was steeped in history. I see you smile.'

'Have another drink, my friend.'

'You're mocking me. You think I'm inventing.'

'No. Not at all.'

'You do. I am not surprised.'

'No, no. Why should you invent. It is a long hot evening, too hot to create. To invent takes energy. It is too hot to create. Shall we agree that you're . . . recreating?'

'I'm not sure I understand your responses.'

'I'm not certain I understand your story.'

Though Manhattan had suggested the further drinks, it was Diogenes who ordered them. When they were brought, he flicked a note on to the bar, to pay for them. It was not sufficient, and the barman had to wait for the unearthing of two silver coins from the recesses of a trouser pocket.

'Had it not been for the sculptress – her appearance; her *reality*; then her ceasing to be there – I'd have stayed in the room, been baked by the heat scorching through the vast sheet of glass, trying to understand the statue, unravel its mystery, persuade myself that its sex didn't matter. There is a beauty . . . there is a beauty . . . When I understand that. When I can encompass that, believe in it, be utterly confident in it without needing to possess, devour it, why then I hope to be content.'

'Contentment? Is that what you're after? When you're content you'll cease to be inspired by beauty, stimulated by it. You won't be set on by it.'

A young man, in a corner of the bar, near to the fireplace, began flicking at the taut wires of a guitar. He hummed softly, inoffensively. He began to sing a song the words and tune of which were so alien to Diogenes and Manhattan that neither was at all affected by the sounds though the music underlined the absurd unreality, the heightened artificiality of their conversation. The two men were pushed closer towards one another as the evening wore on, as the bar filled up. Outside, it was by now quite dark.

'I left the room. I had to find the sculptress. I came out on to the landing. Stood there, listening. I wasn't even aware of the constant sound of the waves. A floorboard creaked, causing me to hold my breath. As I shifted the weight of my body, from resting on one leg to the other, I realised that I had startled myself: the floorboards squeaked again. Otherwise, no sound. I walked downstairs, pausing after each step. I sniffed. As I descended, I put out a finger to touch the banister, to see how thick the film of dust was. Before I had made contact with the wood I withdrew my hand. I'd momentarily forgotten my sticky red fingers, though the substance – whatever it was – was now almost dry. I reached the bottom, stood in the hall, with the front door and porch twenty feet from me.' Diogenes took up his drink, but just before he touched it to his lips he put it down again, though continued to hold it. 'I know nothing external to me occurred at that moment but I turned my head, to the left of the staircase. She was lying there, the sculptress, her legs facing towards the door of the house.'

'She was dead?'

'Oh, yes. I could see at a glance – less than a glance. It had been messy. It *was* messy. I realised then, at that moment, that it was her blood on my hands. There was no reason why it should have been hers but I knew that it was. It made sense. A sense.'

This time Diogenes poured some whisky down his throat. The guitar was now more eloquent, more ordinarily so. There was no improvisation in the song, nor in the music. Though in a literal sense the words were unintelligible to Diogenes and Manhattan they knew instinctively that it was a love song, and that the man would not get the girl. Or, more likely, he would win her heart but then something would go wrong, something that would make it impossible for them to go on loving one another.

'Did they catch the murderer?'

'I think you misunderstand. Who said anything about murder? I don't believe it was murder.'

Manhattan suddenly felt bored again. These amateur detectives.

But the blood? You said it was . . . messy?'

Diogenes laughed, bitterly, it sounded:

'It was very messy. But they didn't find the weapon. It was, the police said, improbable that the fatal wounds were self-inflicted, but not impossible.'

'Why should she have killed herself?'

'Perhaps she knew she could not achieve in the body the perfection she had created in the face.'

Diogenes said this quietly, as if with extreme sorrow. Manhattan remained silent, knowing that Diogenes had spoken the truth. Not that he necessarily believed him, though he had no reason to argue with his words, but because he had said it with a total conviction, a conviction with which it was impossible to disagree. It was, Manhattan realised, the belief of his life, what sustained it, what made it possible for him to go on living.

'I've just realised what your job is,' said Diogenes, as if he had known all the time.

'Even detectives have holidays. Plain clothes can cease to be garments,' replied Manhattan, equally matter-of-fact. 'They never convicted anyone, then?'

'Of murder? No. For her manslaughter I served seven years in their . . . ridiculous gaol.'

Nothing untoward seemed to have been spoken in the conversation, thought Manhattan. He was glad that he hadn't allowed his guard to slip. He despised himself when he lost face.

'How long ago?' he asked Diogenes, once again anticipating the answer correctly.

'Released last week. Been here a few days. Only a few.' He looked down, into his drink.

'Your wife?' said Manhattan, not much concerned with the answer.

'She's meeting me here. Tomorrow, as it happens. I needed . . . a few days on my own.'

'You want to visit the house again, before you see your wife?'

Diogenes laughed, loudly; so much so that a number of

the other customers turned their heads. His laugh had been heard above the music of the guitar, and the singer.

'My friend, my – detective – friend,' said Diogenes, this time with a little sarcasm.

'No, no, off duty, I told you. Just Manhattan.'

Diogenes smiled, about to say something, then decided against it. Instead:

'There would be no point. The statue would not be there.'

'I suppose it wouldn't,' said Manhattan, not really convinced; no more convinced than he had been that it was ever there.

'Dolores?' said Manhattan.

'Oh, her,' said Diogenes, laughing. 'My first girl. Long, long ago.'

He demolished what remained of his drink noticing that Manhattan had finished his. The guitarist was not now singing alone. Most of the men in the bar, and a girl or two, but not the barman, had joined in. The words were familiar to them. This was a bar for locals, it didn't cater particularly for visitors.

Diogenes and Manhattan started to move to the door.

'Would you like a walk before we turn in?' asked Diogenes. 'I know a walk, from the harbour, the pier. Along the coast a little, an inch or so below eye level as you look, half a mile away. A house, out of the village, separated from the other buildings by two fields.'

Manhattan interrupted him.

'But it is dark. We won't be able to see.'

'I know the way. The only route is along the shore, by the sea and scrambling up eight feet when the gardens of the house, which lead down to the sea, are reached. Not that easy. You have to be agile.'

'Especially in the dark.'

They had left the bar, were walking through the main street, down towards the harbour.

'Especially in the dark,' Diogenes echoed Manhattan's words.

'You've done it before?' asked Manhattan.

'That would be telling,' said Diogenes, and they both laughed a little.

· They walked on in silence, looking at the occasional person they passed or who passed them. There were few vehicles.

'Why did you choose here for a holiday – if you *are* on holiday?' said Diogenes.

'If you really want to know, my wife has just left me. She came from here. I wanted to see where she was brought up. I still love Dolores.'

Diogenes stopped.

'Dolores?' he said.

'Yes,' said Manhattan, stopping, looking closely at his face. 'Quite a coincidence, don't you think?'

They walked on, first to the harbour, then along the shore.

12

JANET CAIRD

THE PROJECT

IF it hadn't been such beautiful weather, I might not have gone to Ardronich. But it was a splendid May day, with big white clouds curling up behind the mountains, streaks of snow on the peaks, gold-green in the birches and the heather turning from winter chestnut to spring green. So when I saw the signpost, I thought, 'Why not?' Twelve miles there and twelve back – it wasn't too far and as this was a senti- mental pilgrimage, when I was on leave and not yet actually retired, it would be like going back in time. For the school at Ardronich was the very first I had visited when I came to the Highlands as one of His Majesty's Inspectors of Schools thirty years before.

I remember how remote it seemed, but there had been crofts, two shooting lodges, and at the tip of the peninsula, where an island broke the force of the Atlantic, a little fishing community. Over the years all this had gone. It was doubtful if anyone was left; and the school had long ago been closed. But under the bright May sunshine there was no sadness. The surface of the road wasn't bad, and I drove at a steady thirty miles and thought of Ardronich school.

It was a typical Highland country school; one schoolroom and attached to it the four-apartment schoolhouse, low-set, sturdy, its gable turned to the west and the gales of winter. There was a little asphalt playground, out-door lavatories. In the small garden in front of the house grew low rosebushes, fuchsia, montbretia. The house I remembered only vaguely, though I had tea in the little parlour. But the schoolroom I could remember very well and the school-mistress still better. Not that she was particularly striking-looking. She had thick dark red hair worn in a bun, but her features were a little coarse. Her eyes were a very bright blue and had a curious staring quality as if she were always on the lookout for something. Her clothes were neat but gave the impression of having been chosen purely for comfort and convenience. She was not a particularly attractive woman, and yet she impressed herself indelibly on my memory.

I think this must have been because of the spiders. The first thing I noticed when I entered the classroom was a huge and very well executed drawing of a spider which almost filled the blackboard. On one window-sill there were jam jars containing spiders, and across another window a very clever web had been woven with fine grey cotton. I suppose I looked surprised for she said:

'We're doing a project on spiders.'

I was agreeably surprised. In those days 'projects' were a new, and 'advanced' way of imparting knowledge to the young. To find a project under way in a lost corner like this was quite remarkable. Further questioning elicited the information that she had been introduced to 'projects' at her training college, had been interested, but had not used the approach till she came to Ardronich. There she had found it a good way of gathering all her twenty-two children of varying ages together as a unit.

'Why spiders?'

'We had read Bruce and the Spider, and of course spiders are common creatures and it led on to nature study and hand-work and arithmetic.'

'Very satisfactory.'

The project had not been allowed to interfere with basic learning. The children were well-grounded. They knew their tables (this was still the time when it was not considered an intellectual crime to make children learn their multiplication tables; New Mathematics was as yet but a gleam in the eyes of my mathematical colleagues). I was happy to discover the pupils knew not the meaning of parsing, that most deadening of English exercises, and their written work showed they had been allowed a freedom unusual in those days. Altogether a satisfactory little school.

She gave me elevenses in her parlour while the children romped and shouted outside. She talked intelligently of the countryside, the problems of life in a remote community. She had a collection of books and references in her talk showed her to be widely read. It was clear she could have filled a much more responsible position than being school-mistress at Ardronich. Perhaps there was some personal reason for her being there, perhaps some sadness. As I drove down the road I was aware of a slight uneasiness; as if I had missed something.

I dismissed this as purely subjective, and in my notes written at the Lonliath Hotel gave school and teacher a very good report.

Back in the office in Tynloch, I looked up Ardronich School in the files. Penelope Baxter had come there five years before; the school had been visited once since then, after she'd been there a year. I made a mental note that that was too long a gap; I would visit it more frequently. The report was good; work gave evidence of careful and conscientious teaching; and a start had been made on a project on – spiders. Four years ago. But perhaps what I had seen had been a fresh attempt at the same subject. I asked a colleague who knew the district, what did he know of Ardronich?

'Never been. McDonald – my predecessor – went. Something odd about the teacher. Mad on projects or something.'

'She was doing one on spiders when I saw her. Seems to have been doing the same thing four years ago.'

'Probably you saw the second time round. Can't always be thinking them up. Waste of time anyway when they could be getting on with some straightforward history or geography,' for Duffus was of the old school.

I never did get back to Ardronich, at least not during that spell in the Highlands. After three years I was posted south and remained in the industrial belt for twelve years. From time to time I would find myself thinking of Ardronich and its oddly memorable mistress. Projects were now well in fashion. Every time I met the word or thing I remembered the cotton web on the window of the little school. Then one day, at a conference on 'Linguistics in the Primary School' (grammar having become a dirty word and the pendulum being at the widest sweep of its swing) I had word of Ardronich and Miss Penelope Baxter. One of the younger men – I was out of this category by now – a pleasant chap with a sense of humour and a not-over-dedicated attitude to work – and I were chatting over a whisky before dinner. He was from my old district in the north.

'Tell me,' I said, 'have you been to Ardronich school?'

'Indeed yes. More than once. A strange woman, the teacher. Oh good, you know. The kids learn. But she has a project . . .'

He looked into his glass.

'Spiders?'

'Spiders. But how did you . . . ?'

'She had a project on spiders going when I saw her nine years ago.'

'That doesn't surprise me. D'you know she never completes the project? After four or five weeks she scraps it and begins again. I asked her why, and d'you know what she said?'

'Tell me.'

'She said it began to get a hold on her and if she didn't stop it would get out of hand. Those were her very words. I said, Why spiders? Why not something else? But it was just as if she hadn't heard me. D'you remember her eyes?'

I nodded.

'I thought you would. She just looked over my shoulder and went on talking as if she hadn't heard me; but her eyes went to and fro like the boy's in the *Ancient Mariner*. I'm convinced she's just a tiny bit mad.'

'Surely not.'

'Eccentric, then. But a good teacher, and the children are happy.'

Time passed and in due course I returned to the Highlands as a district inspector, in charge of one of the most beautiful areas in Scotland. As soon as time permitted I went to Ardronich School. Penelope Baxter was still teaching there; the few reports in the files since my own years before were practically identical; 'careful conscientious teaching' etc., and a project on spiders. The two latest reports, however, did say that the teacher had been advised to complete the project and move on to something new.

When I arrived at the school it looked very much as it had done all those years before; the fuchsia bushes were bigger, the montbretia clumps required thinning, the roses sprawled a bit. Penelope Baxter hadn't changed much; the colour of her hair had faded a little, her eyes were perhaps a trifle more prominent; her clothes seemed almost the same. The school-room had scarcely changed at all, except that there were only eight children instead of twenty-two. On the blackboard was a huge drawing of a spider, but there was no longer a web made of cotton hanging in the far window. Instead, real spiders' webs covered it; the deposit of years as it seemed. She saw me looking at it and said:

'We are doing a project on spiders, and I asked the cleaner not to remove the webs from that window. It is not her fault. As you can see, the rest of the room is well-kept.'

And so it was.

I went through the motions of an inspection, knowing full well what I would find – 'careful conscientious teaching etc. A satisfactory school.' The written work didn't seem as adventurous as it had on my first visit; most schools were encouraging greater freedom than Penelope Baxter by this time. I realised the children were writing on exactly the same themes as they had been on my first visit . . . it was as if all the work was confined in a fine web of custom and routine . . . I pulled my wandering thoughts sharply to heel and said abruptly:

'Isn't it time you completed this project and moved on to something new?'

She must have heard these words often enough. One would have expected her to look a little abashed, uneasy. Not at all. She looked away and said:

'I'd like to do it properly. It's not working out quite right. I think I'll start it again.'

And then the pale prominent eyes looked straight at me with a sly and conspiratorial expression. I began to wonder if my younger colleague was right, and if she was not a tiny bit mad. I completed the inspection and left.

Two years later a re-shuffling in the Department sent me to be a Chief Inspector in the Borders, and I was never back in the Highlands in a professional capacity. Two years after I left the north Ardronich school was closed, the roll having dwindled to three. I asked the colleague who gave me the news if Penelope Baxter had ever finished her project.

'I don't know. I told her she must, but the school was closed shortly after.'

'What happened to her?'

'She resigned from teaching, bought the old school and schoolhouse and went on living in it. Apparently she had private means. But there are only two or three families left on the peninsula and they will be moving away soon. So I don't suppose she will be there long.'

And that was the last I'd heard of Penelope Baxter. For years I hadn't even thought of her until I saw the sign-post at the road end.

I was beginning to wonder if after all it had been such a good idea to take the road to Ardronich, for the euphoria inspired by the bright May weather was sensibly diminished by the all-too-frequent sight of ruined and crumbling houses – 'larochs o' auld cottages' – at the roadside. The only indication that humans ever came there were the sheep and lambs, and the slow indignation with which they moved out of the way showed they were used to having the place to themselves. After about five miles I came to a little cluster of tumbling houses, and here I was cheered by the sight of a young man, long-haired, bearded, wearing shabby jeans, who was painting the front of the least dilapidated building still carrying the faded sign 'Ardronich Post-Office'. I drew up and hailed him. At the sound of my voice, another figure, longer-haired, wearing jeans, but not bearded, came out of the cottage, carrying a child and with a bright-eyed toddler clutching her free hand.

'Is it possible to drive up to the old school?' I asked.

The young man was friendly.

'You'll have to walk the last mile or so. But it's in ruins.'

'Still, I'd like to go. I used to know it when it was still in use.'

'Were you a teacher?'

'No. An inspector of schools.'

He looked interested.

'Perhaps you can tell us. Is there any chance of its being opened again? We're hoping to revive the peninsula – get others to come – work the land. And we'll need a school.'

I thought of the ruined houses, the undrained moor, the rocks, the peat. But I couldn't be too crushing.

'It would depend on the number of children and the state of the school. Have you been up to it?'

'No. It's rather far, and . . .'

He looked away and his wife said nothing. The silence grew. I said:

'I'll tell you what it's like on the way back.'

The road was narrow but the surface remained adequate, with a thin growth of grass in the middle. The land was obviously being used for grazing and presumably the road was maintained for the passage of the occasional sheep-float. But quite suddenly it deteriorated and became a rough stony track which ran down into a hollow and then up to the opposite crest where a blotch of low trees and shrubs surrounded the school-building.

I parked the car in the gravel lay-by and set off. At the foot of the hollow the track led on to the ruins of the wooden bridge which I remembered from my earlier visits. As I reached it, the shadow of a cloud filled the valley. The colours were suddenly muted and I saw, half in the water, a drowned sheep, a horrid tangle of yellowing matted wool and white bone. I almost turned back. But it was only a short distance to the school. The track ran up to the hazels and birches that had grown up round it. It would be stupid to turn at this stage.

I edged my way over the planks and went on. Perhaps a little too quickly. When I reached the schoolhouse gate I was panting slightly. So I stood leaning on it for a moment or two.

The garden was a tangle of growth; roses, fuchsia, montbretia, matted together and rank grass choking everything. Part of the roof was off and the rotting beams stuck out like bones. Behind the windowpanes hung shreds of net screens and at an upper window I could see the mildewed back of a dressing-table mirror. So the house was not empty. Inside there were tables and chairs, carpets and china, mattresses and wardrobes mouldering away . . . I turned abruptly aside and made my way through the tangled grass and brambles to the playground entrance.

The iron gate hung askew and half-open. The railings were scrofulous with rust, the asphalt sprouted a rash of green. The door was locked. The windows were set fairly high but I could peer through the lower panes. Inside, the glass was shrouded in a thick material. Cobwebs. Cobwebs matted, thick, dusty; like frail rotting velvet. I went from one window to another trying to see through, and in the gable I found one window where two panes were clear, the webs having collapsed under the burden of grime. And so, pressing my face against the glass, I saw again the Ardronich classroom.

The desks in the centre of the room were dusty but untrammelled. But the cobwebs festooning the walls and ceiling shrouded the furniture at the sides of the room. The cobwebs had changed the shape of the room, rounding the corners, transforming it into a tenuous vault. I could look down the whole length through the strange twilight. I thought I could distinguish a huge spider on the blackboard through the screen of web, but I couldn't be sure, because there was something in front of the board where the teacher's chair had been, a mass of cobwebs spun round some fairly large object – an easel perhaps?

No. Not an easel. My eyes adjusted to the light and I saw. I saw the bony fingers resting on the desk, I saw where the skeleton arms rose to the shoulder-bones; I saw the skull and the thicker web staring from the sockets. Like looking at an X-ray of the body through misty flesh. Miss Baxter of Ardronich had finished her project.

When conscious thought returned I was running down the track, much too fast for an elderly HMI. I remember clinging to the shaky wooden rail of the bridge panting. I remember stumbling up the track to the car, and sagging into the seat and wishing for the first time for years that I had a cigarette handy.

I didn't really see the track as I drove back. The habit-formed, mechanical bit of my mind took over and changed gears, negotiated ruts, steered round sheep and brought the car to a sudden stop at the old post-office. The bearded young man, paintbrush still in his hand, stared at me and said:

'Did you reach the school?'

'Yes.'

He waited.

'Well?'

'Well what?'

'Any chance of its reopening?'

I smiled at him, grateful to him for being there and alive.

'No,' I said, and drove off, leaving him looking after me.

13

ARTHUR YOUNG

STAFF OF LIFE

DURING THE DEPRESSION my father was idle. While my mother worked to keep us he ran a garden allotment, to fill his empty days, to help with food and to salve his self-respect.

It was my job to gather dung.

In the summer mornings while he bent to his weeding and hoeing, I made designs with the white chuckies which outlined the various beds; or made a wee house out of seedling boxes. Come mid-day we ate, sitting just inside the door of the hut which he had patiently built from boxes and old wood.

After dinner, before settling to his only pipe of the day, he would cut the heel and leaf from a stalk of red rhubarb for me. Then he puffed away, while I scrunched contentedly, dipping the end in a little poke of sugar before every bite, grooing in tart delight if I had not coated it well enough.

Soon, when his cronies came by to play solo or dominoes for spent match-sticks, they laughed at me and said it would keep me regular.

Then to be rid of me I was sent for dung, to make the flowers smell and keep the rhubarb red.

I went with Dougie Crawford, the son of one of my father's friends. He was twice my age and had a bogie.

We went to the Stey Brae, to the tracing station. On the way there I got a hurl, hunkering down on the bogie, feet on an upturned shovel. We jumbled over cobbles; swayed round corners; jinked in and out of the traffic, clear across the town to the Brae.

This hill, notorious for its steepness and twists, had running its whole length a pathway of cross-laid granite setts, to help horses keep their feet and give them purchase. At the bottom, the town council had sited a tracing station.

In a stable, by the side of the road, they kept half a dozen powerful horses. On payment of a fee by a carter, one of these would be hitched, tandem, to a heavy load, and the two horses, led by a trace boy, would plod, steaming and snorting, to the head of the hill.

Of course, the stable was a great howff. It was ruled by two ostlers, men with seamed leathery faces, who wore leggings and aprons of sacking. They had ponderous bellies, girt about with broad brass-studded leather belts. They swore at the beasts with hoarse crooning voices; roystering oaths which, I realised later, were really little songs of love.

The place would be full of drivers and carters. There would be joking, and pipe-reek, and spitting, and drinking from quart bottles of ale, while the horses were yoked and loused; fed and groomed.

The traffic on the hill was of all kinds: brewers' drays, coal lorries, grain floats, furniture pantechnicons, contractors' carts – all pulled by big, patient horses, mostly Clydesdales. There was the odd Percheron, Shire or Punch, but they weren't a patch on our local-bred beauties.

Naturally, the six trace horses were Clydesdales too. Our favourite was Hector.

Nobly named, he was the biggest by far, and was superb to see with his creamy mane against his chestnut coat, and his feet, big as pie ashets, with their silky white-fringed spats.

You can imagine our plunder was bountiful. Dougie was on to the droppings in a flash, scooping them into the bogie. Somehow, Hector's offering seemed special, as with utter disdain of the smelly, petrol-driven vehicles all about him, with their stinking exhausts, he lifted his tail and gave out great golden gobs of steaming ordure.

When we returned home, I trotted beside Dougie, holding on to his belt. As we ran we inhaled the sharp ammonia smell of our treasure.

One day a trace boy, sent for tobacco, had dawdled; was not on hand when needed.

The ostler swore.

'Whaur's yon bluidy boy got tae?'

'Can Ah go?' asked Dougie, bold and scared together.

By this time we were kenspeckle.

'Ah believe ye micht!'

Pop-eyed with pride, he took the trace bridle in his hand, then held out the other for me.

'He can come too, eh no?' he asked.

Was there ever such a hero, to remember a halfling like me in that moment of his own glory.

'Weel – ! See and haud oan tae him ticht!'

For, of course, the real reward of being a trace boy was the return journey – on the back of the horse.

We had Hector, our own beauty. He hauled the load to the top with ease, then waited patiently while the carter hefted us up on to his broad back.

Dougie held on to the big leather collar, his knuckles showing white, with me locked between his arms. Greatly daring he dug his heels into the broad flanks. Hector obediently went forward in a slow canter.

We had so often watched the trace boys with envy, that we had never considered the danger.

The huge back was frighteningly high above the cobbles.

The motion was sudden and jerky. The smooth hard coat was as slippery as glass.

Somehow we reached the other end and were helped down. Our terror turned immediately to pride and joy. Our happiness knew no limits at our own daring and success.

So the summer progressed. The flowers never smelt sweeter. The rhubarb was never so red: and I was never so regular.

When summer ended, I went to school for the first time. The allotment was forgotten in November fogs and December frosts.

There was snow, I remember, just before Christmas. One Saturday, late in the afternoon, Dougie appeared in tackety boots and a Balaclava helmet.

'Comin' tae see Hector?' he asked.

'Will I no' just!' I cried.

Without the bogie this time, we dodged along the pavements through the throng of shoppers. The winter wind dirled in my ears and to my intense excitement, before we were long on the way, it started to snow hard. This added the final touch to the twinkle of street lights in early darkness, and the bustle and smells of Christmas. I remember feeling so happy.

Landing on roads already surfaced by packed icy snow, the huge swirling flakes soon formed a muffling carpet. The heavy traffic and the countless feet pounded it hard and slippery. By the time we reached the tracing stable the Stey Brae had been converted into a dangerous glacis, under which the granite setts were buried and useless, despite attempts at clearing and sanding.

We soon caught an anxious undertone to the rough voices for no man wanted to get in the way of the great, pounding, steel-shod hooves as they fought for surety and balance.

'Yin o' they beasts will gang doon afore ye're a' din!' warned one of the ostlers. 'They'll hae tae come aff. It's no' safe ony mair.'

But the carters already there were late and weary and wanted to get done.

'Weel! Yin mair raik an' then it's feenish!' he decreed.

Dougie and I waited confidently beside our bonny giant. He would show them.

He did too.

Stepping like the prince he was, he drove his way up the hill, hauling the yoked horse and load behind him. Dougie and I ran alongside shouting his praises.

On looking back, what made the next happening so horrifying was the incongruous silence. There was no warning horn, no squeal of brakes or tyres, no shout: just the light-beam, grotesquely out of place, shining across the road instead of down as a car slid out of control on one of the bends.

There wasn't even a very big bump, but the momentum and lack of friction underfoot was enough to sweep the cart and the two horses backwards.

For one frozen moment Hector stood his ground four-square, until inexorably his head was pulled up, back and over. At the last moment he tried to roll sideways but his huge frame was never meant for such contortions.

'Christ! The bluidy beast is coupit,' was the agonised shout.

Then the noise started, obscene in its shrill terror. Hector lay flailing on the ground, his teeth gnashing, his eyes rolling in agony, his screams human and mortal. Jagged slivers of white bone sticking from the shin showed where the bone of the leg was broken.

One of the ostlers arrived, purple in the face.

'Aa Christ! Christ! The puir bluidy beast!'

The cry went up for a gun or for the knackers, but shaking his head the ostler drew out a horn-handled clasp knife. Opening out the big blade, he held it cupped in his hand, so that the sharp point lay sheltered and directed along his middle finger. He soothed the pain-wracked animal enough to get near it.

To my utter astonishment he lifted its tail and plunged hand, knife and arm up to the elbow into the pouting dark orifice.

'Whit's he daein' up its airse, mister?' Dougie pulled at a man's coat in alarm.

'There's a big vein in there, son. He'll puncture it, and the beast will soon be quated.'

Then more kindly: 'It'll no' hurt.'

His words seemed true, for a few minutes after the ostler brought his hand away, dripping red, the great horse quietened. His head settled and he began to breathe in ever slowing gasps.

At the end his bowels gave way and skailed a great, reeking puddle of blood in the snow, where it steamed and congealed and turned black.

I felt my head go round.

'Dougie! Take me home!'

I remember nothing of the return trip. Indeed I remember little of the next few months, except that even in those days of tight money, the doctor was called to see me.

The last time I saw Dougie Crawford was just after the start of the war.

He was a pasty-faced private in the Argylls, with black holes in his teeth and a fag stuck on his lower lip. He was killed in Malaya.

The Stey Brae has disappeared. It has been bulldozed,

straightened and smoothed into a gently curving four lane highway. Even now I can go to where Hector died.

I still get rhubarb too; sometimes with custard. But it is pale, anaemic stuff, with chlorotic leaves. They tell me it is produced in some foreign part. No doubt it is forced under glass and fed on chemical concoctions.

It only gives me wind.

14

GEORGE MACKAY BROWN

SILVER

'You'll never get her', said the skipper of the *Kestrel*. 'She's meant for some rich farmer on the hill.' He shook his head.

The three other fishermen of the *Kestrel* shook their heads. 'You're too poor,' they said.

Bert the cook laughed sarcastically.

I took the three best haddocks I could find from the morning's catch and set out for the farm.

They shook their heads after me. The skipper took his pipe from his mouth and spat – he thought I must have gone out of my mind.

I was astonished at my own resolution. Was I not the shy one of the *Kestrel*, who dodged into the wheelhouse whenever a pretty girl stood on the pier above and asked were there any scallops to spare?

I walked on through the village with my three sklintering haddocks.

For the first time – between the tailor shop and the kirk – I felt a flutter of fear. The farm I was going to – it was said that queer proud cantankerous folk lived on it. What could a shy fisherman say to the likes of them, with their hills of green and yellow and their ancestors going back to the days of King Hakon?

That stern tree had lately burgeoned with Anna.

For the love of Anna I was approaching Muckle Glebe.

Old Check was taking the shutters from the hotel bar as I went past. It was opening time in the village.

I stood in need of a glass of rum to feed my faltering flame.

'Well,' said the old landlord, as he set the rum before me and took my silver, 'they're still at it. Belfast. Viet-Nam. The Jews and the Arabs. And now Iceland.'

Poor old Check, I thought to myself, worrying about troubles he can do nothing to put right. How terrible to be old, and your heart as dry as a cork!

'Well,' I said, drinking down the last of the rum, 'but there must be love songs even in places like that.'

He looked at me as if I was mad. One or two villagers came into the bar. I went out.

As I left the last houses of the village the small simple-witted boy called Oik who lives with his mother and three or four illegitimate brothers and sisters in a war-time hut ran after me. The story is that a horse kicked him. If so, that beast set a spark of great innocence adrift on the world.

'O mister,' he said, 'where are you going?'

I said I was going to Anna of Muckle Glebe. No point in dissimulating with a boy like Oik.

'Are you going to give Anna them fish?' he said. He looked at the haddocks with round pellucid hungry eyes.

I said it was a present for Anna.

'Anna's the nicest lass in Norday,' said Oik. 'But she tells terrible lies.'

This mingled estimate of Anna's character, coming from such an innocent mouth, intrigued me. I stopped in my tracks and looked at the boy.

'Besides,' said Oik, 'they don't need fish up at Muckle Glebe.'

The three haddocks flashed in the sun. 'Maybe two would

be enough for a place like that,' I said. I loosened the string and freed a jaw and gave the smallest fish to Oik.

'Now tell me,' I said, 'what kind of lies does Anna tell?'

But he was off. He did not even pause to thank me. His bare legs flickered across the field. The dog leapt out of the hut to meet him, barking. 'O Mam,' he shouted, 'look what I got! That man from the *Kestrel* has give me a fish!'

I went on till I was out of hearing of the sounds of wonderment and barking.

Quite apart from Anna, I was going to Muckle Glebe to get my silver chain back. Anna had taken it from my neck, between kisses, at the dance on Friday night in the community centre. It was the chain my mother gave me on my seventeenth birthday in January. 'Come up to the farm Thursday morning,' Anna whispered. 'They're all going to the mart in Kirkwall. We'll be alone. You'll get your chain back then. And something to go with it far more precious, precious. You can bring a fish too, if you like . . .' And she had sealed the bargain with another marvellous kiss.

I knew then that I could marry no other girl in the world but Anna. The very thought of her, all that week, had been enough to set my spirit trembling.

But how could poverty like mine ever fall like a blessing on that proud house?

My feet went on more slowly.

The shop of Mrs Thomasina Skerry – coats, corned beef, spades, cups, coffee, whisky, salt fish, tobacco, sweets, stamps, newspapers, all in one withered drab hut – stood at the crossroads.

I went in for a packet of fags.

'I like a fish,' said Thomasina, eyeing the couple of slaughtered beauties that swung from my forefinger. I laid them on the floor, out of the way of her all-devouring eye.

'It isn't often we see a Selskay man in this part of the

island,' she said. 'I like nothing better than a bit of boiled haddock and butter to my tea.'

I was talking – I knew it – to the most talented gossip in Norday. Certain information about a certain farm could be traded for a firm fresh haddock, I hoped. (The *Kestrel*, I should explain, visits this island only rarely – we come from Selskay, farther to the west – about Norday we know only rumours and legends.) But, even from the warped mouth behind the counter the very names 'Muckle Glebe' and 'Anna' would come like music: whatever she might say about them.

'I have a message,' I said, 'to a big farm a mile farther on.'

'Muckle Glebe,' she said. 'Muckle Glebe. The Taings – a proud lot. A cut above the ordinary. O, very hoity-toity – you would think they were gentry, or something. Let me tell you, they have their faults and their failings like every-body else. The great-grandfather of the present Taing was an orra-boy, a dung spreader. O, I could tell you a thing or two . . . I haven't been keeping well in my health lately – my stomach – "a light diet", Dr Scott says – "fish, for example", he says.'

'Maybe what you say is true,' I said, 'or maybe it isn't, but there's one member of that family that no tongue could ever blacken, and that's Anna Taing . . .' My lips trembled as I pronounced the blessed name.

Mistress Skerry's eyes widened. 'O, is that so!' she cried. 'Indeed! Anna Taing. I could tell you things about Anna Taing, mister. But I'm saying nothing. It's best to keep silence. In this island the truth isn't welcome. My tongue, it's got me into trouble before now . . . The great thing with fish is that you can use the water you boil it in for soup, and make patties with the left-over bits. The cat, he generally eats the head.'

'What you say,' I said, 'will go no further . . .' And I bent down and freed another haddock-jaw from the string and held it up among her sweetie-jars and loaves and Fair-Isle jerseys.

We admired the beautiful silver-grey shape together for three long seconds.

'Well,' she said, 'I'll tell you. It's general knowledge anyway.'

The fish was hers. She laid it on an old newspaper behind the counter – wiped her hands on her apron – licked her lips – and told me a bad story.

A student from Edinburgh had worked all last summer at Muckle Glebe, from hay-time to harvest. Whenever he got leave to work, that is, for wasn't that little tart of an Anna running after him, from field to byre, and more than running after him once it got dark and the farm work was done. Thomasina had heard it from this customer and that, but she saw the proof of it herself at the Agricultural Show. Hundreds of folk there, going and coming; and there, in the midst of all the people and animals, in the broad light of noon, stood Anna of Muckle Glebe and the student, with their arms tight around one another, and kissing every minute regularly as if to make sure their mouths were still there. Love is for night and the stars. It had been a public disgrace.

But then, Anna Taing was and always had been a man-mad little slut. There was hardly a lad in the island that hadn't been out with her. She would go with any Tom, Dick or Harry. There was that hawker that had been in the island – a right low-looking tyke – wasn't she seen knocking at his caravan door at midnight one night . . .

But she still wrote to this student. She still kept up with him. And the folk up at Muckle Glebe, they were right pleased whenever the typed letters with the Edinburgh postmark came. 'Because, you see,' said Mrs Thomasina Skerry, 'they're a nest of snobs up at that place, and what a grand catch it would be for their Anna – somebody who's going to be a lawyer or a doctor.'

Her rapturous narrative over, she counselled me, whatever my business was at Muckle Glebe, not to breathe a syllable of what she had said.

My throat worked on this gall for a full minute.

'You're nothing but a damned old scandal-monger,' I shouted. And picked up the sole remaining haddock. And made haste to shake the dust of bananas and wheat and cloves and tea and wool from my feet. And left a patch of slime on her shop floor.

At the door of the farm of Muckle Glebe I set down my gift and knocked. No one answered, but I had the feeling that eyes were watching from curtain edges. I knocked again. (Surely there was no duplicity in the true gentle fun-loving heart that had unfolded itself to me at the dance in the community centre – it was impossible – and the world was full of evil old hags.) I knocked again.

This time the door was opened by a young woman – a sister, obviously, and about six sour years older.

She gave me the coldest of looks.

I asked for Anna.

I felt immediately what impudence it was for a common fisherman to come inquiring about one of the daughters of this ancient farm that had a coat-of-arms carved over the lintel.

'My sister Anna,' she said, 'flew to Kirkwall this morning. From Kirkwall she will be flying to Edinburgh. In Edinburgh, for your information, she is to be engaged to Mr Andrew Blair, a veterinary student. It will be announced in *The Scotsman*.'

I mentioned, trembling, a silver chain. She said she knew nothing about silver chains.

She shut the door in my face. When I turned to go, I discovered that the four cats of Muckle Glebe had reduced the firmest and fattest of my haddocks to a jagged skeleton.

15

GEORGE FRIEL

I'M LEAVING YOU

THEY were both in their early thirties. They had no children, and their parents were dead. She was the daughter of a surgeon in the Royal Infirmary, and he was the son of a lawyer. When they were orphaned they each inherited a parental house and some six or seven thousand pounds. They had no brother or sister to share the legacies.

She was educated at Laurel Bank, and he had gone to Glasgow Academy. They met at the university. Their first date was the night he took her to the Rugby Club dance. After a wasted year he stopped idling with beer and billiards and scraped a degree in Economics the year she got an honours degree in French and German.

They married when he began to find his way in the world of business, and she did occasional teaching in her old school. She didn't want a regular job. She didn't mind staying at home. She managed to get a woman to come in once a week to do the rougher chores, but that was all. The rest she did herself, playing the part of a good wife who looked after the comforts of her husband.

He agreed she didn't need to work. They weren't rich, he said, but they weren't poor. By the time he was thirty he had a good post in a big imports-and-exports firm, with his own office and a secretary. They were living in a flat in Kersland Street, but they wanted out of it.

When her father died they sold his house in Giffnock because it was on the wrong side of the river for them. But when his father died too they moved into his house in Bearsden. They liked the place. It had a two-car garage, and they could afford two cars. They thought it would be silly to sell another house just to put more money in the bank, and then go on living in a flat they didn't like.

They had been married seven years when it happened. He was dumb when she told him.

She came out with it one night in April after she had cleared away their evening meal. She marched from the kitchen to the sitting-room and thumped down on her chair. She kept staring at him as if her eyes could send a laser beam through his *Financial Times*.

Her penetrating silence made him peep over his paper. He never said much to her after their first couple of years together, and she never said much to him. Her silence shouldn't have disturbed him. But that night it came over as a demand to sit up and listen. He put his paper on his lap and looked at her patiently. He always paid her the courtesy of listening whenever she had a passing mood to talk to him.

The moment he put his paper down she spoke abruptly.

'I'm leaving you,' she said.

She wasn't smiling and she was quite calm. He couldn't take it as a joke or hysteria. It was a cold statement of fact.

He didn't know what to say or how to behave. He gaped at her, and waited. His reaction angered her. She spoke rather loudly.

'You're not the least bit bothered, are you? You sit there, and I might as well be telling you I'm going shopping in town tomorrow, for all you care.'

'That's not fair,' he said. 'It's just I don't understand. What do you mean, you're leaving me?'

'I mean I'm leaving you,' she repeated. 'Packing up and going.'

'But why on earth,' he started to ask.

He felt she was trying to be dramatic when their life hadn't a script with any drama in it.

'Because I'm fed up,' she said fiercely.

'I see,' he said. But he didn't.

'Is that all you've got to say?' she cried. 'But of course you never have anything to say, have you? My God, you're dull! Dull, dull, dull!'

'I'm sorry,' he said.

He was too shocked to say any more, and she was furious at his humility. She had expected him to make frantic appeals, to argue and fight about it, to be angry and try to talk her out of it. She was as baffled as he was.

He picked up his paper and used it as a shield against her till he thought of something to say. The idea that she would leave him was absurd, yet it terrified him. His retreat provoked her to another attack.

'I'm fed up living here,' she raised her voice again. 'And I'm fed up with you! Your laziness, and your selfishness. The way you sit there night after night and fall asleep on your chair. My God! I daren't contemplate life with you when you're middle-aged.'

'You'll be middle-aged too then,' he said behind his paper, very sour.

'My mind is made up,' she said. 'I'm going. In fact, my case is packed and in my car. I'm going tonight.'

'If that's what you want,' he said.

He saw no use arguing if her mind was made up. He wouldn't go on his knees to her and make a fool of himself.

'My God! Will nothing move you?' she screamed. 'Good God Almighty, are you made of wood?'

'I wish you'd leave God out of this,' he said.

'You sit there like a bloody turnip,' she said.

The remark hurt him. He knew he was putting on weight. He laughed if off by saying all rugby players put on weight when they gave up the game. But he thought it unkind of her to call him a turnip. Worse, a bloody turnip.

'There's no need to swear,' he said.

'You'd make a saint swear,' she retorted. 'A woman tells her husband she's leaving him, and the husband reads his paper and says all right, if that's what you want. What kind of a man are you?'

'I hope I'm too much of a gentleman . . .' he began to answer.

'Oh yes, always the gentleman, that's you!' she interrupted him. 'Never raises his voice or his hand to a woman. All manners and no matter.'

'I was going to say,' he continued, proud to be calm when she wasn't, 'I hope I'm too much of a gentleman to demand obedience from any woman. I respect you – '

'Thanks very much,' she said.

'I have never regarded you as my slave or my property,' he kept going.

'Aren't we noble!' she jeered.

She bounced out of her chair and walked round the room, pulling her fingers. His head swivelled to watch her as he went on talking.

'I've always respected the freedom of women. You know that. If you want to go, and your mind is made up, I can't stop you. You're a free person.'

'You mean I can go and you don't care?' she asked over her shoulder.

'That's not what I said,' he replied. 'I care very much. You've never given me any reason to think you felt this way. But what I feel, what I may suffer, doesn't concern you if your mind is made up.'

She went back to her chair and tried again to make him understand.

'I'm in a rut,' she said. 'I haven't had a holiday abroad since the day we were married. It has always been your fishing and golfing holidays. I'm fed up with it.'

'You've never complained,' he said.

'I'm complaining now,' she told him. 'It's eight years since I was last in Germany, and I've never been anywhere in Austria. The places I've never seen! I'm stuck here in this house all day, and there's not enough in it for an intelligent woman.'

'You could get a job if you want to,' he said.

'And look after you as well?' she challenged him. 'You want me to do two jobs?'

'Other women do two jobs,' he said.

'That's not the point,' she snapped. 'I want away from you, and that's all.'

'Well, if that's what you want,' he said again.

She nearly apologised before she left, as if at the last minute she felt she was treating him rather harshly. She said there didn't need to be anything final about it, she didn't want a divorce or anything like that. But she must have a change or she would go off her head. She would think about it again after a month or two. Then she told him she had got herself a job in a translation bureau, and she had arranged to share a service-flat with Shona McGregor. He was amazed at her duplicity in planning it all without ever giving him a word of warning.

'I'll get in touch,' she said. 'Not at once, of course. But later on. And we can discuss how it's working out.'

'Yes, that's fine,' he told her. 'We'll do that.'

When she left him he went about his work in a state of anaesthesia. Nothing seemed quite real. He didn't sleep well.

He told nobody he was living a bachelor's life again, and he didn't think his wife would go around telling people she had left him because she was bored. Yet it was soon common knowledge. Perhaps he helped to make it so, for he was clumsy in deceit the first time he was asked about her. He was brooding over a drink at the bar before going for lunch in the Malmaison when he was slapped hard on the shoulder. He turned irritably. It was Bob Ramsay, a genial fellow who was scrum-half with him for a season in the university fifteen.

'Hullo there!' he welcomed the intruder.

'Hiya, Jack?' said Ramsay with a grin of manly affection. 'Long time no see, eh?'

They shook hands, agreed it was over a year since they met. When their chat rambled on they bought each other a drink, and then another drink.

'And how's Jean these days?' Ramsay asked at the fag-end of their conversation.

'Oh, Jean?' he said cautiously. 'Well now – Jean – she's gone to her mother for a week or two. Just for a change of air, you know. She's been off colour lately.'

Ramsay frowned at the limp falsehood.

'Back to her mother? I thought her mother was dead.'

'Oh God, so she is!' said Jack. 'That's right. I forgot.'

He splayed his fingertips across his temple, his elbow on the bar. He had meant to have one short drink only before lunch, and now he was on his fourth. It wasn't that he couldn't carry his liquor, but it was the wrong time of day. He felt silly.

Ramsay squeezed his arm, shook it gently.

'Come on now,' he wheedled. 'Tell the truth. You're not looking yourself at all, Jack. You've lost weight. What's going on? Tell me.'

Jack told him.

'I know what's the matter with her,' said Ramsay.

'Yes?' said Jack.

He was eager to listen to anybody who would talk about Jean.

'She's had things too damned easy,' said Ramsay. 'You've been too soft with her. If she had a couple of kids to look after, and no money of her own, she wouldn't act so high and mighty. She's a spoiled girl. Always was. Too much money behind her.'

'Money has nothing to do with it,' said Jack. 'Jean and I were never hard-up, but we were never well-off.'

'That's what you think,' said Ramsay.

'She was never a spoiled girl with me,' said Jack. 'There was nothing she wouldn't do for me.'

'Except live with you,' said Ramsay.

'Well, that's the problem, isn't it?' said Jack. 'It doesn't make sense. I never expected it. I can't think what came over her.'

'You take my Kath,' said Ramsay. He too was affected by extra drinks at midday, and he spoke with foolish pride. 'That girl didn't bring me a penny when I married her. And you know the old man left me a lot less than I thought he had. So Kath goes out to work mornings in a prep school and looks after me and our wee girl and runs the house, and she's too busy to be bored.'

'Good for her,' said Jack.

'Yes, she's a good woman, my Kath,' said Ramsay. 'We pull together.'

'Good for you,' said Jack, but it was more of a snub than a compliment.

'All right,' Ramsay apologised. 'I always say the wrong things, don't I? I'm sorry, Jack. But I do feel for you.'

He wanted to help. He told Jack there was no point going about looking miserable and feeling sorry for himself. He coaxed him to come to a club where four or five old rugby players met every Friday night for a drinking-session. He said they often spoke of him. They still remembered the great try he scored after a forty yards run when he played in a select fifteen against the London Scottish.

The welcome he got when Ramsay took him there was like the kiss of life to a man rescued from drowning. He moved from the dark of loneliness to the light of company. His memorable try was mentioned in the course of the evening and he felt he was a person of some standing among old friends.

He went back fuddled to his empty house. Somewhere in a bureau-bookcase there was an envelope with press-cuttings from *The Scotsman* and the *Herald*. His reborn ego was confirmed when he read again the report that said his try against the London Scottish was 'a thrilling performance'.

'And she called me dull!' he said, swaying. 'Me? Dull? It's not me, it's her.'

His moping days were over. He began to look at the many girls the firm employed. It was, he believed, a purely aesthetic interest in the walk and figure of certain females. Then his secretary went away to look after an ailing father. He was given the smartest girl in the typing-pool as a stand-in. She was young and pretty, and she became very congenial to him. From the way she always hovered at the door before she would leave him, the way she looked at him tenderly, he guessed she knew his wife had left him. Her fond young eyes were silently saying she was sorry for the wrong done to him.

She wasn't the only one who made him feel better. All the girls went out of their way to be nice to him. It gave him a twisted amusement to see people being sorry for him when he was trying to stop being sorry for himself.

He was coping quietly with his new life when a senior

colleague's secretary left to get married. It was a surprise. She had been with the firm for years, and she was turned thirty. Nobody ever thought she had a life outside the office. And because she had given such long and excellent service there was an office party and a wedding presentation, with plenty of drink and a buffet. He was stuck in a corner most of the time with one girl after another.

His temporary secretary came very close, shoulder to shoulder, thigh against thigh. He cuddled her discreetly, his hand squeezing her waist, then under her arm to fondle a breast. She was flushed with sherry followed by gin, and he was carefree with whisky.

The incident made him ambitious, but he didn't start an affair until his new secretary came. She was a beautiful slim brunette, efficient and attentive. He meant nothing by it when, looking at the *Herald* over mid-morning coffee, he remarked there seemed to be a lot of hotels opening round about the city. She read the full-page advert he showed her, and commented on the picture of the luxurious lounge-bar and the dining-room.

'Looks super,' she said. 'I do love a drink and a meal in a place like that.'

To prove he wasn't so dull that he couldn't take a hint he asked her to go there with him and see how the reality compared with the advert.

He behaved very prudently when he took her out. He was no excited schoolboy, he kept telling himself. He could wait and see. He didn't even attempt a good-night kiss when they parted. It was three weeks before he took her at the end of an evening to the bleak house where he lived alone. He started to explain once more about his wife, but she said it didn't matter. She had heard it all already, and she wasn't bothered.

'It's her own fault if you –' she said, and stopped.

'A man like you needs a woman,' she tried again.

She made it easy for him, but he didn't often take her into his house overnight. He didn't think it wise to get involved with a woman working in the same firm, and he had no complaints when, as calmly as she started the liaison, she told him it would have to end. The man she was engaged to marry was coming home from an eight months tour of duty with an oil company in the Middle East. She had never mentioned any man before. He was surprised again how secretive women could be when it suited them.

'I was just as lonely as you,' she explained. 'But I didn't want to say I was engaged in case it sort of inhibited you. You're so moral really. Still, I think we helped each other through a difficult time.'

'Yes, indeed,' he said.

'I don't think I took more than I gave,' she said.

'Oh no,' he said.

When it was all over he was left with a feeling of gratitude rather than affection, and with that experience behind him he was confident he could find another woman whenever he liked.

But he didn't particularly want to start another affair. He drifted back to his bachelor's habits. Every week he had at least one drinking-session with Ramsay and others. Sometimes two or three of them went out on a pub-crawl for the sake of variety, wearing an old suit and raincoat.

There was a touch of daring in it, a quest for adventure. They drank pints from the city centre to the south side or east end, trying pubs that catered for queer types or rough customers.

They knew it was madness, but they enjoyed their pub-crawls and made them a weekly habit.

On those nights he left his car at home and travelled by bus. He was very strict about not driving when he had been drinking. And it was on one of those nights that Jean saw him from her car when he was waiting for a bus home. She was held up at the lights, and there he was, loitering at the kerb.

If he had gone to the bus station she wouldn't have seen him, but his company broke up at a corner where it was easier for him to walk on to the next stop than to go a long way back to the terminus where the Bearsden bus came in. He was so confused after an evening's heavy drinking that he didn't notice he was waiting at a Corporation bus stop instead of the stop for a country bus.

When the lights changed Jean reacted quickly. She made a left hand turn into a sidestreet, left her car smartly, locked the door, and hurried back. She was unhappy at what she had seen. He was rocking there blind to the world, round-shouldered and talking to himself. He looked wretched and neglected.

'What's he standing there for?' she wondered as she ran. 'And that old coat! I could have sworn I gave it away to a jumble sale. My God, he has let himself go. Oh, the fool! And why hasn't he his car?'

She was unhappy enough before she saw him. She was on her way back from Pollokshaws after a visit to an old girl-friend who had a husband and two little boys. Her visit was a flop. The husband disappeared five minutes after she arrived, as if she was a bore he couldn't be expected to endure. And the two little boys clamoured so much for attention that her conversation with their mother was a series of interruptions. She didn't like it. She saw it as proof that even from childhood the male insists on women giving him priority.

She was still in a bad mood on her way back to her service-flat, and she wasn't comforted to think what she would have to put up with when she got there. Shona

McGregor never stopped talking, and she always had to have the radio or television on. It had given her a recurrent headache over the months, and she longed for some domestic peace and quiet. She missed her own corner and the chance to sit down with a book.

Jack was still rocking at the bus stop when she came running round the corner.

'What are you doing here?' she demanded, very strict with him.

'Waiting for a bus,' he said.

He didn't say it as a rude answer to a daft question. He was, as always, polite. He said it with a smile, patiently explaining what might not be obvious, even to a person of her intelligence.

'You're drunk,' she said.

'Not me,' he said, and raised a palm in protest.

'And you need a shave,' she said.

He rubbed his chin with trembling fingers.

'You could be right,' he said.

'Where's your car?' she asked.

'Car?' he said. 'Oh yes, car. Well, you see – '

He couldn't think. She was so severe she frightened him. He saw his drinking-sessions banned, his next affair stopped before it started, and an end to his free and easy hours of coming and going when he pleased.

'I've been phoning you every night for the past month,' she said. 'You're never in.'

'That's right,' he mumbled. 'I'm always out.'

'Oh, stop your nonsense,' she said. 'It's time you – '

'Here's my bus,' he interrupted her, and moved from the kerb to the road, his arm up in a signal.

'That's not your bus!' she called after him. 'That's a Corporation bus.'

He was on it and away, and he raised a hand in a parting salute from the platform.

She ran back to her car. She would drive on at speed and be home before him. He would have a long walk after he left the Corporation bus. She would go in and wait for him and talk frankly. Then she wasn't so sure.

'What if he's not going straight home?' she faltered as she doubled back to the main road. 'And that's why he took that bus. But then, where can he be going at this time of night?'

She drove on, arguing with herself.

'It doesn't matter,' she said in the end. 'He must come in sooner or later. And I'll be there. I'm going back home, back to my own house and my own things, and I'll wait for him. And I'll tell him something. I'll shake him.'

It was only then she remembered that when she left she had forgotten to take her key.

16

EONA MACNICOL

A WELL DESERVED HOLIDAY

THEIR CHATTING is putting me to sleep. Thank goodness I don't have to take any part in it.

'. . . Surely they've got a new carpet since last we were here?'

'I rather liked the old one. Imagine having to carpet a huge floor like this! Must take a large staff to – '

'Your brother's asleep, Miss Gregor. We'd better not talk so loud.'

'Charles! Are you asleep?'

'Leave me alone, Sylvia. Yes. I'm asleep.'

'Don't wake him, dear.'

'Well, if you'll excuse him, Mrs Leitch. He doesn't mean to be rude. Just that, poor Charles! he did get so awfully tired. Almost ill. The parish take its toll of him. Some of the people where we are could do with a permanent social worker apiece. Never out of trouble. And it's apt to come on Charles. One or two of our church members said that to me. "Go away and forget all about Millhead!" one lady said. "Just make him enjoy a well deserved holiday." '

'Better not talk so loud, dear.'

'Oh I doubt if he's quite asleep. Just dozing, I think. Yes, as I was saying, there are some families who are never out of trouble. So demanding. Charles has had a lot to do with one recently. Well not a family; not even a couple really: a young man and a girl. I don't of course listen to gossip, but there's no doubt they're – living together.'

What the gossips are saying. 'Willie Dewar has a girl in with him again. If his mother knew the one half she'd turn in her grave.'

'A slut of a girl. What else could she be? I called at the door with a message she'd left in one of the shops, and what a state that house was in! Clothes all over the floor, and – I didn't look. And a kind of a close smell as if they never opened a window.'

'Look at yon! Isn't she a sicht? Hair hinging all over her face, looking as if it'd never seen a comb far less soap and water. And aye in her slippers. Looks to me as if she's –'

If I listened to gossip I'd never know what to do.

Now Sylvia's heard it. 'Charles! Do you know what people are saying? Willie Dewar has another girl living with him. Not married or anything. I can't understand how a young man of such a decent family should behave like this. He never works – a bad back, he says – always hanging about the pub or the betting shop. Once or twice, did you know? he's been taken up by the police for brawling. And now this. You'll have to speak to him.'

'He hasn't asked for my advice.'

'Now, Charles! It's a scandal. You'll have to interfere. He ought either to send her away or marry her.'

'I'll wait for the right opening.'

I'll look out for them when I go to the shops.

'Good morning!'

'Hiya!'

'I don't think I've met you before. You'll be new to the place? My name's Gregor. I'm the parish minister. May I know your name?'

'Avril.'

'That's a pretty name. It makes me think of spring. What's your surname?'

'Hoch, just cry me Avril.'

'Well, goodbye, Avril. Nice to have met you.'

'Cheerybye, reverend. I'll b' seen ya.'

To be or not to be, that is the question.

'That poor wee thing, I'm heart sore for her. Yon muckle Willie Dewar he's no' giving her a chance. I seen her yesterday hinging oot a line o' his shirts, wi' hands like birds' claws. A clean shirt for his lordship every day, it seems. He winna soil a shirt wi' working, yon yin.'

'She's looking dwaibly, that lover girl o' Dewar's.'

'She's having a bairn. Can you no' tell? It's showing on her. He shouldna make her do all yon work for him.'

'What's she stand it for, if she's no' married to him?'

'She's young.'

'She's feared for him. I wouldna put it past him to lift his hand to her. Especially with a drop in.'

'The fowk next door say there's a shindy many a night.'

'Aye, but they're pretty lovey-dovey too. Kissing and hugging at the window; my good-daughter seen them through the rents in the curtain.'

A ring at the manse door. Sylvia goes.

'It's a young couple, Charles. Two people anyhow. Willie Dewar and I THINK that girl. But she looks different. Hair done and quite tidy. But, Charles, I think – I may be wrong, but I think –'

'Good evening, Willie. Good evening, Avril. What can I do for you?'

'We're wanting to get married, Mr Gregor. I wasn't wanting to come, but Avril, she's been on at me. It seems you spoke to her on the street. She's taken quite a shine to you.'

'Could we be married, reverend? Not in the church, of course. But maybe here? It'd be better than the registry office. You'd say the right words over us?'

'I think you're having a child. I mention it only because I don't want you to think it is in itself a sufficient reason for marrying. You ought not to marry unless you really love one another. Willie, you've had other girls in before.'

'This is the only one now, Mr Gregor. I promise you. I really do love her. I want to get married. I'm needing that to steady me.'

You're needing something certainly.

'Could we, reverend?'

'Avril, how old are you?'

'I'm coming on eighteen.'

'And your friends, my dear? Where are your family?'

'I havena got what you'd cry friends. I was brung up in an orphanage. My mammay ran away when I was wee. I never kennt my dadday.'

'I want you both to think carefully about this step. It's for life, you know. Or should be.'

'Aye. But I canna wait that long. My suit'd be ower ticht. I've a braw new suit, purply pink with pink excessries. And pink platform shoes. The shoes'll keep, but no' the suit, 'ken.'

'We'll think about it. Mustn't be in too great a hurry.'

'Charles, have they gone? What did they want?'

'They wanted me to marry them.'

'No! Did they?'

'Are you surprised? You said they ought either to marry or separate. Well, they want to marry.'

'I'm surprised they should ask you.'

'Why? I'm the parish minister. They have the right to ask me. They want a proper marriage. At least, the girl does.

You must allow people to have some grace in them, Sylvia, whatever wrong things they do.'

'Yes, yes, I know. She's rather an attractive little thing, isn't she?'

I can't think what it is she reminds me of.

Here's Avril. I was hoping not to meet her.

'Hiya, sir!'

'Hullo, Avril.'

'Please, sir, when are me and Willie to get wed?'

To be or not to be?

'I'd like to see Willie once more, alone. You must tell Willie to come and see me alone. Maybe then, in a week or two – would that do you?'

'I've let my skirt out as far as it'll go.'

'I'm glad you've come, Willie. You must take time and think before you get married. Do you really love her?'

'I'm crazy about her.'

'Well, but I mean, will you be kind to her?'

'How d'you mean, Mr Gregor?'

'Oh – take care of her. Carry the coals in, make the breakfast any morning she's not up to the mark, don't expect her to do too much washing and ironing for you.

'And don't bully her. Do you hear me, Willie? She's not very big, is she?'

'No. But she's a right wee tartar too. She knows how to stick up for herself, big or no big. She's got a temper like myself.'

'Well, but she's much younger than you are. Also she hasn't had the good upbringing your mother gave you. So you must be kind and understanding. Gentle. Not lose your temper. You know what I mean.'

'I love her, Mr Gregor. Better than any of the ones I've

had before. I'll settle down. You'll see. You'll marry us,
won't you, the way Avril wants? She says she doesn't want
to get married any other way.'

I have my doubts about you yet.

'Tell you what, Willie. I'm going on holiday. As soon as
I get back I'll come and tell you definitely if I feel I can do
it.

'There is, of course, the child to think of.'

'Aye, there's the child. I don't want my bairn born out of
wedlock.'

'You're right, Sylvia. She is having a child.'

'Then of course they must marry. For the child's sake.'

Lo, children are a heritage of the Lord: the fruit of the
womb is his reward. As arrows are in the hand of a mighty
man, so are the young children. Happy is the man that hath
his quiver full of them.

Sylvia won't be pleased I've said I'd do it in the manse. I
know how it will be.

'Really, Charles! What right have they to expect it? I'll
have to get the house spick and span, and it isn't Mrs Smith's
day. And flowers – I suppose I'll have to put flowers in?'

Willie has a red carnation in the buttonhole of the dark
suit which he wore at his mother's funeral with a black tie.
He is accompanied by a young man I don't like the looks of.
He's had quite a bit for a start. And Willie is not quite sober.
I hope he isn't going to try to kiss Sylvia! – Here, after them,
comes Avril drunk with joy, and her best maid who has two
toddlers at her heels. Sylvia may fuss about the children,
they're dropping icecream. Avril looks simply terrible in
that tight glossy suit. She ought to have worn a loose coat.
She looks awfully sweet though, with her golden hair done
up in a pile and a chaplet of flowers round it. Makes her face

minute. Ah, now I know what it is she looks like: it's Bambi. The curve of forehead and nose are just his. Her birth certificate says she's seventeen and three-quarters, but she looks more like fourteen.

All the time I put them through their vows she pants slightly. 'That they may live in holy love until their lives' end.'

They ask Sylvia and me to the reception, but in a tone which says we'd be better not to go. A drinking session in the Shovellers' Arms, I imagine.

What's done cannot be undone.

'IT'S NOT DONE YET!'

'Charles!'

'Don't wake him. He must have been having a dream. He's gone to sleep again. It's good for him.'

They ought to marry for the child's sake.

'She's a wee beauty, reverend.'

'What a big baby for such a tiny mother!'

'Guid gear gaes in little bulk, eh, Mr Gregor?'

'Hullo, Willie! The proud father. Congratulations. I'm very pleased. What are you going to call her?'

'If it'd been a boy we'd ha' cried him after you. But it's a wee lassie.'

'You choose a name for her, reverend.'

'Let's see. What about Alison?'

'Why Alison, if it's no' a bold question?'

'Oh I don't know. It's in a poem I used to like, about spring. Your name comes in too.'

> Betweene Mersh and Averil,
> When spray beginneth to springe,
> The little fowl hath their will
> On their songe to sing.

An hendy hap I have yhent,
  I wot from heaven it is me sent,
From all women my love is lent
  And lit on Alysoun.

Bairns, they're no long in growing.
  'Hiya, peoples!'
  'Hiya, hen! See you and no fall off of that gate.'
  'She's a right taking wee body, that Alison of the Dewars! What a cheeky wee face she has, with that turn-up nosie and a saucy look in her een. Hear at her singing!'
  'She hasna a care in the world. Content wi' hoose and faimily.'
  'Willie's real good wi' her. Would you ever have said there would be such a difference on a man?'
  'And Avril, she's grown that sensible. She's aye busy with her bairn, dressing her and playing with her.'
  'The pair of them, they're that quiet and douce, the pollis is never near the house now.'

O hush thee, my baby, thy sire is a knight,
  Thy mother a lady, both lovely and bright;
The gooseberries, rasps and blackcurrants we see,
  They all are belonging, dear baby, to thee.

*

O fear not the siren, though loudly it blows,
  It calls but the pollis that guard thy repose.
Their whistles would splinter, their truncheons be red,
  Ere the step of a mugger drew near to thy bed.

As arrows are in the hand of a mighty man, so are the young children. Happy is the man that hath his quiver full of them.

But the children, are the children happy?

Lead me, Lord! Make thy way plain before my face.

'That Dewar woman, she winna keep the place clean. It's dishes in the sink and pans on the flair and bairns' mess everywhere.'

'Willie should ha' kenned. He should ha' kenned she didnae have it in her.'

'It's Willie's fault. How can she keep the place clean wi' bairns outside o' her and a bairn within?'

'All thae bairns – and God kens who's the faither and who's the mither o' the one half o' them. The one's as bad as the ither.'

'If you ask me, they should never have got wed at all.'

Lead me, Lord.

'Those Dewar bairns, they're just rinning wild. Yon wee Alison, if she doesna look eftir them nobody else will. She's aye off the school racing to the shops then back for to cook something for them. The attendance officer is eftir them for it, and so he should.'

'. . . Into folks' gardens, breaking windows, lifting this and that. If you so much as check them, the language you get'd make your hair stand on end. Where do they hear such dirty talk as this?'

'They must learn it off of their father. For their mammy's gone. Beat it.'

'I'm no surprised their mammy's up and left them.'

'Why did she leave you, Willie? What did you do to her?'

Adam, where art thou?

'Somebody said she had a black eye. Were you rough with her?'

'Me, Mr Gregor?'

'Yes, you.'

It's taking too big a risk to marry them.

'They'd ha' been best getting quit o' each other at the very start. They shouldna ha' married because o' the bairn. What's one bairn? They could ha' put her into an orphanage. She'd ha' had a better life of it in any case. What sort of a home is that for a young lass to grow up in? Put her in an orphanage and be done with it.'

> I'm nobody's child, I'm nobody's child.
> I'm like a flower, just growing wild.
> No mammy's kisses and no daddy's smile.
> Nobody wants me. I'm nobody's child.

'I want to go home. I want my own place. I want to climb on my own gate.'

> O hush thee, my baby, thy sire is a knight,
>   Thy mother a lady, both lovely and bright.
> The gate and the swing and the doorstep we see,
>   They all are belonging, dear baby, to thee.

*

> O fear not the shouting, though louder it grows,
>   It is but thy parents, as everyone knows.
> Her boyfriends would vanish, his greyhound lie dead,
>   Ere their punchings and kickings should fall on thy head.

'My mammay's out with her pals. And my dadday's at the pub. But they'll be hame, the baith of them, before it's my bedtime. They'll be bringing in fish and chips to our supper. I'm to make the toast and the tea.'

'But how are you managing, Alison? All the other children?'

'Hoch, the bairns is OK. I've Charlie in his bath and Sheila's bedded. My dadday'll likely be bringing us icecream.

Mammay and dadday and me, we'll sit round the fire and scoff it. We have wir fun, 'ken.'

'How's your mummy these days?'

'My mammay's fine. She has to bide in the house now. There's another wee yin coming. My mammay and my dadday are real pleased. They're painting the cot and getting a brand new bath for it. That's four of us you'll soon be baptising. My dadday's coming to see us getting done.'

As arrows in the hand –

'And I'm top of my class. And I'm to be a flower girl in the Gala Day. I'm going to have a dress that comes down to my feet. One of the ladies in your church is helping my mammay to make it. My dadday gave her two pounds for the cloth for it.'

'He's a great one for his bairns, that Willie Dewar. I'd never ha' thocht he could change this way. A family's steadied him up. And him such a rake before!'

'He's that keen to work, he never misses a shift.'

'He and Avril, they're settled and happy. It's grand to see them.'

In holy love until their lives' end.

'Are you happy, Avril?'

'Aye am I. It's the first time I've ever had this kind o' life.'

'We want to get married, reverend.'

'I want you to think carefully about this step. You must be kind to her, Willie. You must carry in the coals. And keep your temper, keep your temper, Willie.'

'I'm crazy about her.'

To be or not to be?

Yes, I will do it. If you never took any risks –

'YOUR ATTENTION, PLEASE!'

'Poor old Charles, they've wakened you up properly this time.'

'What a shame!'

'PAGING THE REV. CHARLES GREGOR. WILL THE REV. CHARLES GREGOR PLEASE COME TO THE OFFICE FOR THE TELEPHONE? REV. CHARLES GREGOR FOR THE TELEPHONE, PLEASE.'

'That's me!'

'Gracious, yes, that's you, Charles.'

'Whatever will it be?'

'Well, don't just stand there, dear. Go along. I do hope it isn't some tiresome crisis in the church. It'd be too bad of them to bother you on your holiday.'

I'm sorry I can't stop, old Mrs Somebody. I can't wait to listen to your question or make you hear the reply. 'I'm going to the telephone, Mrs Mhmhm. The telephone. Yes, that's right.'

I can't take it in.

It isn't real anyhow.

The very people I've been thinking of?

The carpet is soft and deep. It would come up like moss between my toes if I had bare feet. I remember the sphagnum moss where we went climbing when I was a child. When I was a child. When I didn't have anything like this to cope with.

'Charles!'

'Here we are, Mr Gregor! You're going past us. Here we are.'

Lord, thou hast been our dwelling place in all generations –

It can't have happened. It isn't true what I've just been hearing. I must have made a mistake.

'Charles, what's the matter with you? You're all white and shaking.'

'I'm quite all right, Sylvia.' Leave me alone, will you? Just this once.

'He must have got up too suddenly. I often turn giddy when I get up too suddenly.'

'What was the phone call about, Charles?'

'It's Willie Dewar. And the girl.'

'What about them? He hasn't had the cheek to ring you up and try to get you back from your holiday in order to marry them?'

'It wasn't Willie on the phone. It was somebody else about Willie. About Avril.'

'What about them?'

'I can't explain now. I'll have to go. He's asked for me.'

'Back to Millhead? Now?'

'Yes, right back to Millhead. I mean, to Edinburgh.'

'Has something happened?'

Yes, something has. 'They're in a bit of trouble.'

'But can't it wait?'

'No. I'll have to go now. No, Sylvia, I don't want you to go with me.' It'll be bad enough going alone. Very very bad.

I remember seeing that house with the dovecot in the garden. I remember the way the ivy grows over the wall, only now I'm seeing it from the other way round. I remember that milk bar with the bin for waste paper in front of it. Sylvia made some remark about it ages ago, two days ago, ages. This corner looks just the same. Only it must be different, everything's different.

What could I have done to prevent this?

I'll have to see him. He's asked me to come. There's no escape. I'm going at sixty miles an hour to him. I'm running down into the Forth valley. I see the pylons of the Bridge.

O for the wings, the wings of a dove,
   Far away, far away would I fly.
   Far away, far away, far far away, far away would I fly.

'Remanded in custody.' I've often wondered what that meant. Shall I say 'Willie Dewar' or 'Mr William Dewar'? I don't have to say either, they seem to know. They politely give me a chair, but I can't sit down.

They're taking a long time. It must be he doesn't want to come.

Adam, where art thou?

What is this that thou hast done? The voice of thy fiancée's blood crieth to Me from the ground.

O Willie, poor Willie.

'It has happened, has it?'

'Aye it's happened. I don't know how. We'd both got drunk, 'ken, and something she said got my temper up. I can't mind what it was. I hit her with the bottle I had in my hand and she fell. And that kind o' angered me more. So I went on hitting her. I couldn't stop. It's like a dream the way I mind it.

'My lawyer's putting in a plea of self-defence. He says didn't she maybe hit me with her handbag or something. But that can't take this feeling I've got away. What'll I do, Mr Gregor?'

My punishment is greater than I can bear.

'You asked for me, Willie.'

'Will you go and see her, Mr Gregor? I'm not allowed.'

'What good will it do?'

'Just if you would go and see Avril for me. Tell her – tell her – I don't know what to tell her.'

'She can't hear anyhow.'

'But go all the same. Will you? Somebody that knows her's

got to see her. Tell her I'm real sorry about the baby. What'll I do, Mr Gregor? What'll I do? I wish I'd never been born.'

How can a man be born when he is old? Can he enter a second time –

'All right, Willie, I'll go. Where she is she'll forgive you.'

A cold clean place. She looks like a sleeping princess in a fairy tale. So still – you'd never guess she'd had to die that way. They've put a tactful wimple round her head. Only her face shows. She's more like Bambi than ever, that curve of forehead is just his. There's a rounding of the draperies over her belly. God, God! I mustn't laugh now. I've seen pregnant brides before, but never a pregnant –

> I thought thy bride-bed to have decked, sweet maid,
> And not have strewed thy corse.

'I've a braw suit, purply pink with pink excessries.'

'She's a wee beauty, reverend.'

'You choose the name.'

I'll have to bury her.

But it can't be yet. I haven't the strength yet. I'll have to try and remember the words to say.

Hear my prayer, O Lord, and with thine ears consider my calling: hold not thy peace at my tears. For she was a stranger with thee, as all her fathers were. O spare her a little, that I may recover my strength –

That can't be right?

I'll have to clear my brain. I'll have to walk about, go somewhere, till I clear my brain.

'Hiya, peoples!'

'Hiya, Alison.'

'Hear at her singing!'

O hush thee, my baby, thy sire was a knight,
    Thy mother a lady, both lovely and bright.
O God, whose nature and property is ever to have mercy
and forgive – Lord, have mercy upon us.

Where am I? And who are they all? What are they saying to
me? What a din they make. It's beating on my brain.

'Who's here, hinging on to the gate?'

'It's the minister, begosh, Mr Gregor.'

'Aye, it's fearful things has been went on here, sir, two
nights syne.'

Christ, have mercy upon us.

'Are you wanting for to see where it happened?'

Not particularly, thank you.

'He's standing there, hinging on to their gate. Is he having
a seizuar? Go and take hold of him, Jock.'

'Me? I'm no a member.'

'Go, one of you. For he's muttering to himself. It's as if
he's went gyte.'

'He isna weel. It's a shame he's had to come away like
this from his holiday.'

17

JULIE DAVIDSON

FOOL ON THE HILL

SHE FELT self-conscious but amused as soon as she got out
of the car. Sitting on the dyke was a middle-aged couple,
seemingly eating thermos flasks and plastic boxes, and they
watched her with cool curiosity. Where were her friends,
where was her husband, where was her boyfriend on this
fine Sunday-boyfriend afternoon, where was her little dog,
guarantee of good intentions? Young women did not walk
alone on the isolated plug of an impotent volcano, even
when the fire is gone from its belly and its sore old sides are
soothed by a dressing of grass and gorse. Young women
who walked alone in lonely places invited rape and murder,
and probably deserved them.

She smiled to herself, picturing the tramlines of their
minds, twin tracks conducting them comfortably to a
common terminus, and then she turned her attention to the
hill. Even from this angle, close to its roots, it was almost
symmetrical; no untidy hill, confused and dissembled by the
shoulders and arms of a dozen neighbours so that you never
knew where one ended and the next began. It was a no-
nonsense hill, even aggressive in the way it asserted its
volcanic soul by jumping straight out of the ground at the
bottom and ending where you expected it to end at the top.
She looked up with a small, swelling feeling of intimacy,
making her first overtures of reaquaintance, nervous of

change and reassured by the path between the sunbursts of gorse and the allegorical look of its rabbited turf.

The couple on the wall were still watching her, so she stopped to stare for a long time at the willow tree over the burn so that they could marvel further at her eccentricity. The tree had been important. *My foot is on my native heath, my name it is MacGregor and from this mighty willow I will leap the roaring rapids to escape the cursed enemy.* She considered the idea of saying the words out loud for the benefit of Picnickers Anonymous, but decided that would be the action of a true eccentric, or even a psychotic. She had a duty to her sanity at the moment – to considered action, balanced judgment, rational decision. But she also had a duty to the child who had once crouched in a sad old willow tree and with the bright, permissible insanity of childhood turned a muddy trickle into MacGregor's Leap.

The child tugged at her. The hill pulled her upwards. She went joyfully, vigorously, slipping off her sandals and coupling her bare feet with the turf, shaking the wind from her hair like water. There was a child who had a habit, once, of pushing out her under-lip and blowing the hair from her eyes; a child with a dog who was teased while he slept and jerked and grunted in his dreams when she blew on the pads of his feet. Gently, teasingly, through a diffusion of light and wind and sudden sound from ambitious larks and the rhythmic stretching of her own muscles, the hill released her memories like a slow feed of adrenalin to the bloodstream. I am getting higher and higher, she thought. My energy is inexhaustible. Perhaps I shall have a peak experience on the top of this hill. But she refused to look back at the view and concentrated, instead, on each pull of oxygen from the well of the wind and the placing of her feet.

I have this thing about hills, she was fond of saying to friends. I have this thing about getting to the top of them . . .

once I start I can't stop, I must keep going until I reach the top. Of course – bright, self-mocking laugh – I'm sure it's all terribly Freudian. There was a child, too, who always wanted to be Rob Roy and never just a clansman, and the first in her class to jump from the highest diving board, and the one to demonstrate, from instructions given in *The Observer's Book of Ponies*, how to pick up the Shetland's foot by his fetlock and inspect it for stones. Only the child had never heard of Freud and the desperate, self-indulgent, cocktail-party misapplication of his theories.

She allowed herself a pause and a circumscribed glance left and below, knowing what she would see: black tufts of fir like a false beard on the fields and a seductive slice of water. On cue it dripped another memory into her mind, and she saw herself describing it in terms of infant sexuality to her friends in the city. (Her friends in the city, busily offering her fashionable advice, busily recording for the documentary of their times their separate conflicts of urban alienation or cultural demoralisation or sexual role confusion or spiritual loss or perhaps just the agony of the middle-class housewife who has been trained to use her mind and not look after children.) Children in a forbidden forest, after tadpoles in a bottomless reservoir, and after some privacy, too, where they thought they might kiss each other: 'If you're my boyfriend, William, then you ought to kiss me.' But the excitement at the taboo reservoir was reserved for tadpoles, and they leaned over the concrete sides to fill the jam jars with the jam of their spawn and carried them home through the close dark trees like proud parents. 'We forgot to kiss each other,' she said, when they were back on safe pavements. They would do it another time. Did they? She couldn't remember. A playful little question presented itself to her. If a woman forgets the boys who have kissed her, does an old woman forget the men who have made love to her? Stupid, stupid question. Angry, she ran on and away from it, clutching at grass with her hands and the wind with her mouth . . . Oh God, don't let me start on that lost innocence trip.

The energy of the prayer thrust her up the path, dampened her eyebrows and the hollow between her breasts and made her conscious of them. *Belle poitrine,* she had been told by a man who found it easier to use French for his intimate moments; and with the air ballooning her lungs and her eyes on the lumpier breast of the hilltop she could really believe that they *were* beautiful, and that it counted, as if they contained some kind of cipher to her personality. Perhaps they did now. That thought skeetered dangerously on the edge of a decision, but it wasn't time yet and she resented it. She ran on in a passion of sudden optimism, an optimism of the body which strengthened as she climbed as if, like the giant Antaeus, she grew in power with each touch of the earth. The sounds of her body performing their functions kept time with her movements and arranged themselves into a small chant:

There's a kettleful of blood singing in my head
There's an automatic door opening in my lungs
There's an air-compressed hammer pounding at my heart
And small sharp heels stamp the pavements of my veins.
The city of my body gets things done for me
But sometimes I don't like to live there.

Would anyone else like to live there? Do they decide or do I? Too soon, too soon. She collapsed on a shelf of turf and let her marching song drain from her mind and let the sun shine in. The sun was always her undoing. She wished she could reach up and hold it like a lover; she wanted it inside her filling her with a shower of gold; she wanted the sun and the grass, the grower and the growing, to meet in her middle and resolve something there. She concentrated on hot red light and gritty green texture and her skin sensing the air like a different element.

'Couldn't stand that film,' said her voice, brittle with violent, disproportionate distaste. 'The director went berserk with all that heavy pantheistic symbolism during the sex alfresco. All those swaying trees and ridiculous orgasmic bursts of sun through the clouds. Couldn't stand it.'

It was true, she couldn't stand the film. She had closed her eyes against the pain of its lyricised emotions. She had become faint with recollection, re-routed tears running in her throat, projecting her own lost joy on to the celebration of the celluloid lovers and finding it returned as physical anguish. Even now the memory of memories made her stir sharply on the grass, her body automatically clenching and her senses seeking distraction in a different kind of joy, re-focusing on the shrill, shameless choral symphony taking place on the updraughts above her. That film director would have loved those manic larks, pulling themselves upwards on their own vocal chords, tripping over the top to the tune of their pre-arranged ornithological programme.

It was the music lesson. She was caught out in a lie, the first public lie. 'For this, this is Flora's holiday, this is Flora's ho-o-o-o-li-day.' She could still remember the tempo and the quavers and the Arcadian purity of the words; a classroom of little girls singing to open windows and the sounds of summer. But she had grown tired of nymphs and shepherds, written a note of disgust and thrown it to a friend across the passage. The piece of paper dropped between them, and the teacher saw it. 'You threw that, didn't you? Is there anything written on it?' And that was when the lie happened. 'No,' she said. Such an honest, decent little lie, contained within herself and hurting no one. Strange that there is only one kind of lie for children. Strange that they have no concept of self-deception. It must

be a learned skill, like learning to sophisticate the unsubtle
childhood acts of betrayal like the one which exposed her
lie. 'There IS something written on it, Miss. I saw her
writing.'

The lie released, brought forth from the safe cell of her
private conscience to be tried in open court. Oh God, I do
believe, I really do believe I have never felt such shame and
guilt since. What has happened to all my guilt? My guilt was
beautiful, but they have wiped me clean, the space-age
saviours. My sins have been expiated by the rationalism of
liberal, progressive, humanitarian intellectuals. The pulp-
mill philosophers and the electronic evangelists have
swopped my own small daily crucifixions for their global
guilt, and a problem aired is a problem shared is a problem
spared. Give me back my OWN guilt! The world is too light
a load on my mind.

The world, her world, would willingly absolve her if she
decided to exercise the adult privilege of self-deception. She
got to her feet. There were rain clouds on the sky's edge
now, and she watched the weight of them silently bruise
the skin of other hills. Her own hill still waited, her body
was calm for the last short climb but she didn't really
believe there was much more either could tell her. Still, she
had this thing about getting to the top of hills. I feel I could
almost meet myself on this path, she thought; a little girl
with big freckles and big ideas and too busy to know me,
running too fast to recognise the woman she's going to be
some day. Are we such strangers after all?

On the top of the hill, the wind pulled her about in a
sudden glad game. She sat on a rock and picked a pink
blossom of clover to nuzzle while the sky and the land held
her between them. She waited, watching two figures climb
the last stretch of path. It was the picnickers, the Sunday
censors from the car park. The man straightened and saw

her and gave a gasping grin, sensing solidarity in common achievement. 'Is it worth it?' he called.

The wind delivered her answer. 'Oh yes, it's worth it all right.' She hugged her stomach with her arms and added silently, 'I've climbed all this way to tell my baby that.'

BIOGRAPHICAL NOTES

GEORGE MACKAY BROWN was born in Stromness, Orkney, and has lived there all his life apart from a few student years in Edinburgh. He began by writing verse but has recently moved more and more to prose. His second novel, *Magnus*, was published last autumn. Two books are scheduled for 1974 – *Hawkfall* (short stories) and *The Two Fiddlers* (Orkney legends for young people).

JEREMY BRUCE-WATT was born of Scottish parents in Calcutta in 1929. Reared in Scotland, he left school at sixteen to become copy boy for an Edinburgh newspaper. National Service as an infantry corporal included reporting for an army newspaper in Greece. Spells in a London factory, on a Lowland hill farm, and as a television journalist in Glasgow varied a newspaper career which ended in 1973, when he left journalism for full time writing. He is unmarried, and lives in Edinburgh 'for the time being'.

TOM BUCHAN was born in Glasgow in 1931 and educated there and in Aberdeen. He has published three books of poetry and also works as a playwright and theatre director, best known as co-author of *The Great Northern Welly Boot Show*. He was Professor of English at Madras University in the fifties, Warden of Community House, Glasgow, 1958–60. Until 1970 he was Head of the Department of English at Clydebank Technical College. At present he is Editor of the Scottish monthly *Scottish International*.

ROBERT BUCKIE was born in the port of Grangemouth less than thirty years ago and sought his education in various wood-yards and Universities here and abroad. Being a few stamps short of a decent unemployment allowance he decided to emigrate and the coin turned up Canada. He now lives in what he calls the Golden Oxter of Ontario and is glad to say that he retains his native dialect despite the efforts of school, television and posh people.

JANET CAIRD was born in Nyasaland (now Malawi), and educated at Dollar Academy and Edinburgh University. After graduation she studied at the Sorbonne and Grenoble University. She is married to James B. Caird, District Inspector of Schools for Ross and Cromarty, and lives in Inverness. She has published one children's book, *Angus the Tartan Partan*, and five novels, *Murder Reflected*, *Perturbing Spirit*, *Murder Scholastic*, *The Loch*, and *Murder Remote*.

DEIRDRE CHAPMAN was born in Carnoustie, Angus, in 1936, and has worked for various newspapers in Glasgow and in London. She now writes a weekly column for the *Sunday Mail*. She is married to journalist Michael Grieve, whose father is Hugh MacDiarmid. They have three sons and live in Glasgow.

JULIE DAVIDSON was born in Motherwell, Lanarkshire; educated mainly at Aberdeen High School for Girls; started writing short stories while still at school; runner-up and winner of the *John O'London* short story competition for the under-21s in successive years when 17 and 18. Then stopped writing fiction to go into journalism with D. C. Thomson. Joined *The Scotsman* in 1967; lives in Edinburgh's Royal Mile.

ELSPETH DAVIE went to school in Edinburgh, trained at the College of Art, and taught painting for some years. Lived for a while in Ireland before returning to Scotland. She has published a collection of short stories, *The Spark*, and two novels, *Providings*, and *Creating a Scene*, the latter winning a Scottish Arts Council award.

GEORGE FRIEL was educated at St Mungo's Academy and Glasgow University. Worked in various jobs before becoming a schoolmaster. Enlisted in the army, and served in the RAOC for five years. Resumed a teaching career, but recently gave it up. Has written for radio and television, and published short stories in a handful of defunct magazines. Has also published five novels, *The Bank of Time*, *The Boy Who Wanted Peace*, *Grace and Miss Partridge*, *Mr Alfred M.A.*, and *An Empty House*. Scottish Arts Council awards, 1969 and 1972.

GILES GORDON was born and brought up in Edinburgh. He now lives in London with his book illustrator wife and three children. His latest publications include: *Girl with Red Hair*, novel; *About a Marriage*, novel; *Walter and the Balloon*, juvenile. He is at present co-editing an anthology of New English Writing and a book about Jury Service.

EONA MACNICOL was born at Inverness. She has spent a good part of her life in India, where she taught English in a college. Now lives in a mining village near Edinburgh with husband who is parish minister. Two sons and one daughter. Has published historical novels on the life of St Columba, and a collection of short stories set in Loch Ness-side, *The Hallowe'en Hero*.

NAOMI MITCHISON was born in Edinburgh and now lives in Kintyre. Was for many years member of Argyll County Council and started their travelling art collection for schools. As member of the Highland Advisory Panel got to know most of the Highlands. At present member of Highlands and Islands Consultative and Development Council.

ROBERT NYE, born in London in 1939, is a free-lance writer who now lives in Edinburgh with his wife Aileen Campbell, and their children. Since 1962 he has been leading book reviewer for *The Scotsman*, and their Poetry Editor since 1967. His publications include: *Darker Ends* (poems, 1969); *Doubtfire* (novel, 1967); and *Tales I Told My Mother* (short stories, 1969).

ALAN SPENCE was born in Glasgow. Writes mainly haiku and short stories. Published in various magazines and broadcast on Radio 4. Scottish Arts Council Bursary 1971. Since 1970, he and his wife have been disciples of Sri Chinmoy, who has given him the name Janaka.

PATSY THOMSON the twenty-seven year old daughter of an Irish father and English mother, was born in Nottingham but moved to Glasgow six months later. She went to school locally then took a degree in modern languages at Glasgow University. After graduating she taught in a Glasgow primary school and now concentrates most of her energies on caring for her two young sons and lecturer husband. She has an abiding concern for the welfare of Partick Thistle Football Club.

FRED URQUHART's first published story appeared in 1936; his first novel *Time Will Knit* in 1938. Since then he has published two other novels and nine volumes of short stories, including his Collected Stories in two volumes (*The Dying Stallion* and *The Ploughing Match*) in 1967–68. He has worked for a literary agency, film companies, and has been a publisher's reader for over twenty years. He edited *Scottish Short Stories* (Faber, 1957). He has a new collection of stories ready for publication, and is finishing a novel, the first of a projected series of five about a Scottish brother and sister.

ARTHUR YOUNG is the pen-name of a Scottish family doctor. Educated at Hamilton Academy and Glasgow University. Now practises in a New Town. Lately come to serious writing and encouraged by the appearance in 1973 of this volume. Has now completed a novel and is at work on two more.